COLD BLOOD

MARNIE VINGE

For all of us that say we'll put our true crime binge-watching and binge-listening to use some day

ONE

I SWEAT from the heat of the studio lights. Sitting in my uncomfortable armchair, I cross my legs and place my palms on top of my knee as one of the makeup artists does last-minute touch-ups to my face.

In my peripheral vision, I see another makeup artist doing the same to Erika Lam.

Erika is one of the most famous anchors in broadcast history.

She's interviewed presidents, dictators, Olympic athletes, movie stars, and pop stars.

Anyone who is anyone has been interviewed by Erika Lam.

The thought that she would be interviewing me today about a book I wrote is overwhelming to say the least. I didn't set off down this path thinking that it would lead to fame or anything resembling that.

No, you don't get into something like this for fame.

It's a nice byproduct, though. The more awareness I can raise, the better.

"You look good," the makeup artist says. I smile at her, having forgotten her name and feeling terrible about that. I just nod, unable to find words.

I'm suddenly wishing that my psychiatric service dog, Ghost, wasn't back in my dressing room resting, and instead here by my side. I should have brought him out with me.

I glance over at Erika, hoping she doesn't see me, taking surreptitious looks at her. I feel like I'm in the presence of someone truly great. A journalist that I looked up to when I was younger.

I bite my lip and then immediately remember, I have lip gloss on. It's something I don't normally wear.

I press my lips together, trying to correct whatever damage I might have done by biting it, cross my legs, and straighten my blouse. It's navy blue. Far more expensive than anything I own.

I tried my best to get them to dress me as I normally might. Which is to say completely casual and without any frills.

But apparently that wasn't good enough for Good Morning Today.

The pressed blue shirt is stiff against my skin. I can feel the starch. It practically holds me upright, correcting my bad posture.

I look out from the stage and see everyone taking their places.

The makeup artist finishes with Erika, who says nothing to me. She just stares straight forward and I take a cue from her doing the same.

Finally, one of the guys behind the camera starts counting down from five, and when it gets to one he simply holds up a single finger.

And then we're live.

Erika speaks with that same presence I've come to know over the years. She puts it on as easily as trying on clothes.

"We have a special guest here today. Josephine Larson is an investigative journalist. She has spent the last year interviewing none other than the Heartland Hunter serial killer, Nathan Kelly, and her recent book about him has become a New York Times bestseller. *Nightmare on the Trail: The Heartland Hunter,* a book that was created after extensive interviews with serial killer Nathan Kelly at a maximum security prison in Colorado. Without further ado, how are you doing today, Josephine?"

Erika turns her attention to me and I freeze.

The studio lights are so damn bright and it's so quiet in here, I can hear my heart beating.

She smiles at me, giving me an encouraging nod, begging me to speak, and I find my voice.

"I'm doing well," I say. "Thank you for having me today."

This is just like any other interview, I tell myself.

Even though this one's a lot bigger. This stage is a lot bigger. This audience is a lot bigger.

But Erika does her best to put me at ease.

"Congratulations on your book sales. I think that this is a topic that many Americans are very interested in, particularly women. I find it interesting that women seem to be the biggest consumers of true crime. And you yourself have spent a long time in the company of a serial killer that specifically targeted women. What's that been like?"

"Well," I say. "I have a theory about that. I think a lot of women have an obsession with true crime because we are the primary victims of serial killers. The primary victims of violence, with the statistics being even higher for people of color and the LGBT+ community.

"Listening to these podcasts and watching these shows about grisly murders is a means of protecting ourselves. We want to educate ourselves about the thing that poses the greatest threat to us. When a woman goes on a date, she tells her friends where she's going because there's a chance she might not come back. When men go on a date, they don't do that sort of thing, at least not to the same extent. They don't think twice about asking to pick you up at your house. Many men who mean well come off as creepy by trying to be nice, but women have to think about those things. And I think that's why we have an affinity for true crime.

"We've heard too many stories about women that were picked up for a date and never seen again. Or who left their drink with a guy and went to the bathroom, only to wake up with no memory of the night. The world is a different place for women than it is for men. And I think that's why women gravitated to this book. To the true crime community as a whole. As far as what it's been like interviewing Nathan Kelly, it's been enlightening in a very dark way. Learning how this person thinks and views the world. How he views women, in particular.

"Learning that not everyone feels the same kind of empathy that you do is jarring at first, but I did my best to keep an emotional distance between myself and Kelly."

"That must have been hard, considering your personal connection to one of his crimes."

"Incredibly," I admit.

"I think that's something that gave a unique spin to your book," Erika says. "The fact that one of the victims was your friend's mother. And that the two of you were camping with her when she went missing."

I nod.

"Was Nathan Kelly aware of that when you were interviewing him?" she asks.

This is the part I was dreading. "He was. At first, I didn't feel that it would do anything but make my interviews with him more complicated. And I didn't want him to be able to exploit that point of vulnerability."

"Did he try to manipulate you?" Erika asks.

"He tried very hard," I say. "But I kept a firm wall up with him for the most part." Though there were times I said too much. "And I think that the study of serial killers is necessary. If we're ever going to advance psychology to the point that we might be able to pinpoint the signs early that someone might become one of these dangerous individuals."

Erika nods as I speak, like she's taking every word very seriously.

It's a gratifying realization.

Sometimes I'm not sure if there is value in what I did. Sometimes I think that maybe I'm just a ghoul, staring at a sideshow.

"It seems like you would have to keep that emotional distance," she says. "This had to have a very personal impact for you, writing this book. Has your friend read it?" Erika asks.

I freeze.

Jordan hasn't read it, though she told me I was doing the right thing. For a moment, the studio disappears and I'm in the woods. I'm grabbing her upper arm so tightly that it leaves a bruise the next morning.

I clear my throat and come back to reality.

"She hasn't read it," I say. "But she gave her blessing."

"It's probably a hard thing for her to read," Erika says.

"To say the least," I remark.

In a way, it's not my story to tell. But I was there. And more people need to know about what happened that night. One day, I think it might make a difference.

"Have you always had an interest in darker things? Beyond your personal connection to this?" Erika asks.

"Yes," I say. "Ever since I was a little girl, about eight

or nine years old," I go on. "I loved R.L. Stein's *Goosebumps*. I loved *Scary Stories to Tell in the Dark*. I couldn't get enough of them. My favorite thing as a kid was when my dad would tell us stories around the fire. They were always about monsters and ghosts, that sort of thing. And I think as I grew up I realized that those aren't the monsters we need to be worried about. It's the monsters we meet in our everyday lives. Real flesh and blood humans are the monsters, and that's the scariest part of all of this. They can look like anyone. They can be anyone. It could be someone you know, someone you trust, even. These people often lead double lives," I say.

"What was it like the first time you met Nathan Kelly?" Erika asks. "Did he look like he could have been just anyone?"

I still remember the first time I set eyes on him.

He looked me up and down, like I was a snack to be devoured. He used my first name. We'd talked on the phone prior to that, when he'd agreed to be interviewed.

In that moment, I knew he'd looked at each and every one of those women that way.

The thought was chilling.

"He looked like he could have been anyone," I admit. "But there was something about his presence that made me uneasy."

Nathan Kelly had the blackest eyes of anyone I've ever met. His irises were such a dark brown that his pupils were indistinguishable from them.

It gave him this demonic look.

And when he laughed, it completed the image.

"He spoke to me about his crimes as so many of these people do: without any sort of emotion. The strongest feeling I think any of them have when they're recalling these events is pleasure. I think they find it enjoyable to go back over their crimes with people who want to interview them. That's one of the disturbing parts of writing this book. He liked telling me what he had done to women. He liked seeing my reaction. And at first I did react a lot. I tried to keep that at bay when interviewing him, to not let him know that the things that he'd done were scary to me.

"But sometimes it's hard. Especially with a criminal like Nathan Kelly."

"It should be," Erika says, holding up my book for the camera. "There are many descriptions of Mr. Kelly's actions in this book that would be disturbing to some. It is said that he is the most gruesome serial killer the United States has ever seen. I would caution anyone who is going to purchase the book to be aware of that. Josephine has not altered his descriptions or censored them in any way. It's a difficult read, but very well worthwhile.

"Thank you so much for being here," she says, turning to me. "I think the work you've done is noble."

I don't agree with her.

I just smile and nod. And then I thank her.

"We'll be back right after this," she says into the monitor and then someone yells "To commerical!"

I relax, realizing that I've been holding my body as

rigid as humanly possible this whole time. Only breathing enough to answer each question. I realize I'm sweating under my arms ferociously.

"Thank you so much for being here," Erika says to me off camera.

I nod and thank her for the opportunity.

But there's still a part of me that feels like maybe I'm no better than PT Barnum, leading people to the sideshow to look at the freaks.

I'm not a forensic psychologist.

I'm an investigative journalist.

One of my biggest skills is getting people to talk.

Something about me disarms them. Maybe it's that I'm small, blond, blue-eyed.

I look like I could be the girl next door.

There's nothing about me that's intimidating.

Probably unlike the FBI agents and psychologists that the government sends.

I think Nathan Kelly enjoyed talking to me. And the whole while I was talking to him, I never quite got out of him exactly what I wanted.

I stand up from my seat and I'm ushered back to my dressing room.

They thank me for being on the show and I thank them again for the opportunity. And then I'm left alone to gather my things. Ghost is just where I left him, as well-behaved as ever. When I tell him to settle, he lays down and doesn't move from that spot until I tell him to.

The television is still playing in the dressing room,

broadcasting a commercial in between the segments on Good Morning Today.

I pack up my things and stuff them into my bag. I just brought a backpack. Hardly professional. I change out of the clothes that they gave me back into the ones that I left in the dressing room. A t-shirt and jeans.

It's then that Erika comes back on the air and I glance up at her, wondering if I was really just interviewed by someone that I've admired for a really long time.

Her face isn't gleeful though.

There's a strain in her look. And I listen as she speaks.

"We've just been handed a breaking report that a young woman has flagged down help on an Alaskan highway in a remote part of the mountains. The woman was nude and reported being held by a man she believes to have been a serial killer. She is being interviewed by police and they are not making any comment right now," Erika says.

"Talk about relevance," her co-host Amy Potter says.

"Indeed," Erika says.

Amy touches my book on the desk.

"This sort of stuff is relevant now more than ever," she says.

I stare at the screen with a sinking feeling in my gut and look at Ghost, still resting in the corner. He pops his head up now, though, and walks over to me, pawing my leg, to let me know that my heart rate is speeding up.

TWO

I SIT THERE, staring at the breaking news on the TV in my dressing room. This can't be. It's too similar to the way Kelly's last victim was found. She escaped and told her story. It was shortly thereafter that he was caught at a campground. She'd seen the color, make, and model of his truck, plus the first three letters of his plate.

This could be a coincidence, I tell myself. But there's a little niggling doubt that makes me think it isn't. Headlines are sometimes deceiving, I remind myself.

And at this point, it could be anything. It doesn't have to be what I'm afraid it is.

There could be someone else out there taking inspiration from Nathan Kelly right now. That's the most likely thing. I think about how, recently in the news, BTK said that someone was killing just like him, drawing inspiration from him even.

They think of themselves as artists. As people who are actually contributing something of value to the world.

I watch the TV until the screen changes to something else. Another headline chasing this one right out of its prime spot. The news moves so quickly, it's hard for anything to get a spot for long. And that's probably the last we'll hear of this, I assure myself. Maybe it's some misunderstanding.

There's a knock at my door.

"Come in," I say.

The person on the other side gingerly pushes the door open and reveals themselves to be one of the production assistants that I met earlier. I smile at her.

"Miss Larson," she says. I remember that her name is Patricia. She's way too young for a name like that. But maybe she's an old soul, and maybe her mother knew that when she was born. My mom always said as much about me and my name, but I think it had more to do with the fact that my father had wanted a son. He always called me Joey. My mother hated it.

My father spent my childhood trying to shape me into the son that he had wanted. Anytime we were out, and I asked for a doll, he would suggest something else, maybe a truck or a toy from *Jurassic Park* if he had the extra money. Anything that was less girly.

When I was little, I never really picked up on it. I just found it annoying that I couldn't get what I wanted. I loved the *Jurassic Park* toys and the trucks because they came from my father, but I always wanted other toys.

Barbies. Baby dolls. He even dressed me like a boy. He was always picking out t-shirts and jeans that looked as genderless as possible. I was a tomboy growing up, and slowly I became more interested in things that boys liked. Like video games, and all of that. And that was something that my father seemed to approve of, like it had been part of his master plan all along.

So, I always feel a little twinge of annoyance when someone calls me Miss Larson. It feels too feminine, and in a way that makes me feel very vulnerable. Maybe it's the work that I do, knowing that these men take advantage of women in every way possible, in every situation that they can exploit.

"I was just getting my things," I tell Patricia. She smiles at me.

"You did great," she says.

"Thank you," I tell her. "C'mon, Ghost."

Ghost gets up and positions himself directly beside me, carrying his leash, and I take it. He's such a beautiful dog. A Swiss shepherd, all white, and just as intimidating as his German cousins.

She seems to hesitate before what she says next, like she's thinking it over.

Finally, whatever it is gets the better of her.

"I just have to tell you that I read your book and you're amazing," she says. It all comes out in one rush. She doesn't take a breath between any of the words.

I smile at her, grateful for her compliment, but entirely undeserving of her kind words. I'm not amazing.

"That's very kind of you," I say.

Patricia looks horrified.

"I mean it," she says. "You really are great, and I admire you so much. Someday I want to get out of here, and do what you do."

I fight back a bitter laugh. I want to tell Patricia that she definitely does not want to do what I do for a living. Or encounter the kind of people I have over the last few years. But I smile, trying not to appear ungrateful for her words.

"I hope you get an opportunity to do what you want to do soon," I tell her.

She smiles at me, blushing. And then the two of us and Ghost walk out together onto the street where she thanks me once again for being on the show and tells me that she'll pursue her dreams as soon as she can.

When we leave each other, I wonder why she would want to pursue something so dark. In all the people I've come across who do this sort of thing, they all seem to have a single thread that ties them together. Some dark experience that sparked their interest in the horrible side of human nature. Or maybe a wrong from the past that they feel they can right by studying this stuff.

I try to tell myself it's not that deep, and not everyone interested in serial killers has some secret, horrific personal reason for being interested in them. I think a therapist would tell me I'm projecting.

I hail a taxi cab, and in New York City that's easy.

Immediately I slide inside and Ghost gets down in

the floorboard at my feet, curling up in a ball that's impossibly small. I tell the cabby that I need to go to the airport. He makes short work of the drive. A flight to California is waiting on me. I'm headed to San Quentin this afternoon. Another interview, another killer. The book publisher wanted me to try my hand at doing a follow-up to my book about Kelly.

I watch out the window as we travel across the city. The ride is easy and my driver doesn't try to make small talk, which I appreciate. I don't think after being interviewed that I could take another round of questioning, even if it only has to do with where I'm going and how my day has been.

I busy myself on my phone. Looking at my calendar.

Today I have an interview with James Stanton.

It's just an event in a Google calendar, completely innocuous to anyone who would be looking at it. But the guy is a serial killer, and a pretty notorious one at that.

He was a truck driver, known for picking up girls at truck stops, telling them he'd give them a lift to the next one. He always acted like he wasn't interested in their prostitution services. But the truth was he just wasn't interested in paying. He, like so many other serial killers and like Nathan Kelly, has a deep hatred for women and he enjoyed exacting violence on them.

James Stanton is over 6′4″ tall and he weighs about 300 pounds.

I don't think he's ever been interviewed by a woman, especially not someone like me.

Compared to him I'm tiny, probably a lot like the women he assaulted in his time on the road.

There has been a rash of bodies found along I-40 over the last decade or so. The FBI even has a page on their website dedicated to it. Dedicated to the idea that there might be a long-haul truck driver who is a serial killer. And more likely than that, several of them.

Interviewing James Stanton might give me a bird's eye view into the mind of someone who might be doing those things. And it might be valuable to my contacts at the FBI. I've been lucky enough to get in the good graces of some of the guys there. Some of the teachers that work in the profiling area of criminal behavior.

There are others there, though, that don't appreciate what I do. Think that I am a sensationalist and I'm only out to make a quick buck. But they know better than anyone there's nothing about this that's quick or easy.

I close my calendar app and look up seeing that we're passing through the tunnel that leads us to New Jersey. It's only about a quarter of an hour later that I'm being dropped off at the airport. I thank my driver, and Ghost and I get out. All I've got is my backpack that's got a couple of changes of clothes. I carry a second bag for Ghost with his food and everything he needs. I hand him a tip, and he smiles, thanking me. After I shut the passenger door, he drives off.

We head inside and check in going through security, and go through all the motions that are required to get on a plane these days. It's not long before we're at our gate, and I have a couple of hours before my flight to California.

Ghost sits at my feet, and I decide to pass some time on social media.

That immediately turns out to be a bad idea.

Front and center of my social media page is a picture from *National Geographic*. That wouldn't be a big deal to anyone else. It's a picture from Ukraine. A child crying in the rubble of the fighting that's going on there right now. The photograph itself is moving, and I would be struck by it anyway. That's the whole reason I tap on it to open the whole post. But it's the name I see in the caption credited as the photographer that stops me in my tracks.

Robert Copperweight.

It's like the breath is sucked right out of my lungs. I know that name better than I know my own, probably, and there it is in black-and-white. He feels like a stranger now because he is. Someone that used to be an integral part of my life is now just someone I used to know who takes pictures for *National Geographic*.

I bite my lip, fighting back the urge to throw my phone across the gate, smash it into a million little pieces with all the anger I feel towards Rob.

He left me at the moment I needed him the most.

I can still feel those little rubber grippers sticking to the floors as I moved through the hospital hallways. And he was nowhere to be found.

I close out of the post and scroll quickly past it. I think about blocking NatGeo's Facebook page.

I scroll back up to their post and snooze the page for 30 days.

My heart rate starts to return to normal, seeing his name has triggered me. But then the posts get more mundane. Updates from friends about their kids, summer break, and the things that they're doing. A hiking group I'm part of has several posts from different national parks, people enjoying their vacation time. My blood pressure is starting to return to normal when I see an article about the woman found today on the side of the highway in Alaska. I tap the post and before I can start to read it I see the comments.

Every other comment mentions Nathan Kelly by name.

It shocks me a little bit to see that. The fact that people would already go there. But on the other hand, it doesn't. It's so common for people to jump to the assumption that anyone could be a serial killer. If there are more than two dead bodies found in a river in any given city, true crime groups all over Facebook go crazy.

It shouldn't be surprising that they're already linking Nathan Kelly to whoever was holding this girl hostage.

It's as I'm looking through the comments that my phone starts to ring, a little notification popping up at the top with a number I don't recognize. The area code is one that I do, though.

Virginia.

I pick up the phone hesitantly.

"Hello?" I say.

After looking through those comments, I have a sinking feeling in my gut about where this might be coming from.

"Is this Josephine Larson?" It's a man's voice that I don't recognize. I confirm that it's me. "Hi," he says "this is Special Agent, Lucas Parker."

I don't recognize the name, but it confirms my fears about where the call is coming from.

There must be more information than what's being shared on the news.

"Congratulations on your interview on Good Morning Today," Special Agent Parker says.

"Thank you," I say simply, knowing this conversation is going somewhere that I'm not sure I want to go.

"I imagine you have an idea of why I'm calling," Parker says.

"I have a suspicion."

"Are you at the airport?" he asks.

I confirm that I am.

"We'll get a ticket for you to Fairbanks," he says. "There's something going on up here that they want you to take a look at."

"Is this about the woman that was found today?"

"I'm afraid it's more than that," Parker says. He goes on. "Another woman has been found along the same highway. It looks like the two might be related. The woman who came running out of the woods this morning had a zip tie on one of her hands, and the woman who was found beside the road dead also had a zip tie on her hand. Normally, we don't involve journalists, as you know, at this point, but you know more about Nathan Kelly than probably any other person on the planet. And it looks like this guy might be taking his inspiration from Kelly."

I sit there stunned. Parker speaks again.

"The flight to Fairbanks leaves in an hour. You're already at the airport so that shouldn't be a problem. Will you be able to join us?" he asks.

I feel myself falling deep down into a hole. And at the bottom of that hole is Nathan Kelly looking up at me with those dark eyes. The blackest eyes I've ever seen. I imagine myself face-to-face with him again. That first meeting. I can still feel the warm flesh of his palm when I shook it.

I hesitate for a moment, knowing that I can turn this down. But that's not true.

Because that's not who I am.

I don't walk away from the darkness, I run into its arms.

And I have a bad gut feeling about this that maybe I'm right about something I don't want to be right about.

"I'll be there."

I look back down at my phone after I hang up, the image taken by Robert burned into my mind. I think about where he might be right now, and I think about when I first met him.

THREE

AFRICA FELT like an alien planet where my mother didn't just die.

Thousands and thousands of miles from home, I felt safe for the first time in years. The news station sent me here, worrying that it would be an imposition in the middle of my grief, but it was a lifesaver. In Africa, I felt like a different person. Not Jo. Not the girl who just buried her mother.

The funeral was tiny. Less than ten people came, a testament to a life lived at the expense of others. My dad didn't even show up, not that I expected him to. It had been years since we'd even spoken. I didn't have a working phone number to call and tell him that Mom had died.

Sitting on a wooden box outside my tent in Kenya, all of that seemed like another reality. The break was welcome.

The news station had sent me here because of a story about the Oklahoma City Zoo lions. They wanted to make a documentary for the zoo to be able to play in the lion exhibit. So, I found myself camping near a game reserve in Kenya. Despite the sounds of lions and elephants at night, I was getting some of the best rest I'd had in years.

"Want some instant coffee?" Matt, my camera operator, asked me as he walked up beside my tent.

"Usually, I wouldn't say this, but yes," I told him with a smile as I looked up at him.

After he went to make coffee for me and some of the others, he came back to discuss filming for the day.

"So, basically, Ronald is going to take us out to get some footage of the lions." Ronald was one of our guides. From South Africa, he'd moved to Kenya to study lions. "We're going to interview George when we get there." George was another lion expert. Both of these men carried rifles on themselves at all times which certainly made me think that maybe there were more risks than I realized on this assignment..

"I'm ready," I told Matt. I'd spent the previous day refining some questions for the interview.

As exciting as going to Africa was, this was scarcely hardline journalism. Because of that, I felt like something was missing. All the time I'd been working for the local news, I'd longed for something more. No doubt, a local journalist can make a difference, but I wanted to be on the biggest stories possible. I wanted to cover more dangerous things. I wanted to make an impact on the whole nation with my voice and the truth.

That morning, after I'd slogged my way through barely drinkable coffee, we set out with Ronald. He drove an open-top Jeep like so many of the people who worked on the reserve. He drove so fast, the little dusty trail in front of us weaving through trees and bushes, some of them reaching out and scraping my right arm as I rode shotgun.

"Shit," I'd hissed when a particularly sharp one got a hold of me. I pulled my arm back into the Jeep.

"They'll get you," Ronald said above the sound of the vehicle.

"I see that," I told him.

We traveled a few kilometers into the game reserve. On the way we saw some gazelle, an elephant, and various birds, all of whom had plenty to say about our arrival in their territory. The elephant didn't seem particularly bothered by us, but I wasn't naive enough to think he would enjoy our company up close. I'd done my homework, watching as many videos as I could get my hands on about Kenyan wildlife and how to survive an encounter with it. I knew our guides had rifles powerful enough to take an elephant down, but I wasn't keen on getting in any situation where they might need to use them. It was making me both anxious and excited that we were going to be conducting the interview in front of some lions that weren't in any sort of enclosure.

Ronald slowed the Jeep down as we approached two

figures in the distance. Two lions. One of them was a male and the other female. The male's mane came into view quickly. The female lay under a tree while the male stood up and stepped forward toward the dirt trail we would take if we were driving right past them.

Ronald stopped about fifty feet away.

My heart beat faster and my palms grew sweaty. The nerves I'd had only moments before were replaced by something else: exhilaration.

Ronald stopped the Jeep and killed the engine. The two lions watched us, the male not taking his eyes off of me. The female licked her paw, looking like a large house cat. They were stunning.

The male had scars, surely marks from fighting other male lions for his position over his pride. There were several on his haunch, making me think that another lion had gotten ahold of him. The female had scars, too. Though I imagined hers were the result of hunting the large game that called Africa home. I wondered how violent those encounters could become.

"He could snap your neck in two seconds," Ronald said, bringing me back to reality. "We should get on with the interview."

I finally broke my stare, meeting Ronald's eyes and then Matt's in the back seat. We all remained in our seats.

I asked Ronald about the ways that the Oklahoma City Zoo and the game reserve had worked together. We talked about the future of lions in Africa and the future of zoos in America. The questions I asked were softballs. This was a piece meant to make people feel good.

Just as George was beginning to answer some questions, there was a sound behind us.

The snapping of a branch and a low growl.

The male lion.

I turned quickly. He bared his teeth at us, letting us know he was in control of this situation. He took several steps forward, quickly and with purpose.

"Hey!" Ronald shouted, waving his arms over his head. Then he looked at me. "Get in your seat."

I slipped down into the passenger seat and reached back, pulling Matt into his even though he was in the process of getting a shot of the lion. George slid into his seat, too. Once we were all in our seats, Ronald popped down into his and turned on the Jeep.

The big cat roared and jumped forward, throwing himself onto the hood of the Jeep.

"Shit!" I shouted, bracing myself against the door, preparing for the impact of one of the lion's paws against my skull. As scared as I was, I couldn't look away. The lion's teeth were a yellowed bone and saliva strung from lower canine to upper canine on one side. His eyes were wild, an apparent sign of how far he was willing to go to get us away from his pride nearby.

I pressed myself against the back of the seat and the door. Ronald threw the Jeep into reverse and hit the gas, slamming the pedal into the metal floor of the Jeep. The engine roared and the tires spun, quickly ejecting us from the scene. The lion hung on for three or four seconds, finally letting go and falling to the ground. It quickly got up and continued stalking toward us at a lope.

"Turn around!" George shouted from the back seat.

Ronald performed the most effective three-point-turnaround I'd ever seen, and we were off.

I turned in my seat, bracing my hand against the driver's side headrest. The lion had stopped and now stood in the middle of the trail, watching us disappear into the distance.

I glanced at Matt and both of us shared a grin and then began to laugh.

"Weren't expecting an adrenaline dump?" George asked from the backseat, making his voice heard above the whir of the engine as we tore back to camp.

"Not quite that big of one," I admitted. "Do the lions often chase you?"

"They've been more aggressive as of late," Ronald chimed in. "They're contending with poachers. They have to be on guard all the time now."

Poachers. Now there was a story.

I relaxed back into my seat for the ride back to the tent.

FOUR

BACK AT CAMP, we sat around the fire that night telling stories. We swapped adventures from different assignments that we'd been on and the guides told us some of their own harrowing tales involving the big game of Africa. Apparently, it wasn't always the lions you had to watch out for.

Other people had camped nearby and by the end of the evening, I'd caught wind that one of them was a photojournalist. He caught my eye sitting outside his tent, hunched over his laptop that night, looking at pictures he'd gotten from whatever adventures he'd been on earlier in the day. He was handsome. Very tall and broad-shouldered. He looked like he worked out, not to look good, but because his lifestyle demanded it. I wondered what kind of things he'd seen, and when curiosity got the best of me, I went over and asked him.

"Josephine," I said, sticking my hand out. "I'm here for an assignment from a news station in the States."

He looked up at me like I was the most curious thing he'd ever seen.

"You're not the usual type I meet out in the field," he said, shaking my hand. He had an Australian accent. I'd be lying if that didn't automatically make him more attractive. "I'm Robert. Robert Copperweight."

"Nice to meet you," I said. "What brings you to the game reserve?"

Robert looked up and around, sizing up the crew I had with me, all of them gathered round the fire with the guides.

"Poaching," he said.

For a second, it didn't register what he meant. He laughed.

"I'm covering it. I'm a photojournalist."

"Oh," I said, suddenly feeling more than a twinge of envy. "What's that like?" I asked, sounding more inexperienced than I'd have liked.

"Frustrating," Robert said with a sad smile. "There's not much I can do to stop it other than take pictures of it. Raise awareness. Hope that I can get the story out to the biggest platform I can. I'm going to show this one to my contact at NatGeo. I've worked with them in the past."

National Geographic. Wow. I was impressed.

"That's a lot more impressive than what I'm doing out here," I told him. "I work for a news station in Oklahoma. We're doing a piece for the Oklahoma City Zoo and a little special that'll run one evening on the local channel."

Robert looked up at me.

"You seem bored at the prospect of that," he said.

"You're observant," I said with a laugh.

"Hardly," he said. "It's written all over your face."

I laughed.

"Good to know. I'll try to hide my disappointment more during my next interview."

"Or you could come with me for the day," Robert suggested, looking at me with a smirk. "Do some real investigating."

"Oh, really?" I asked, trying not to show my hand. I very much wanted to take him up on the offer. A small voice reminded me that this guy was a perfect stranger and I was thousands of miles from home in a foreign country. It should have been common sense. It should have been an easy *no*.

"Yeah, why not?" Robert asked. "It's going to rain tomorrow," he said. "I doubt you'll be filming outdoor interviews in the rain. Come with me instead."

"Okay," I found myself saying before I could think better of it.

"It's settled then," Robert said. He stood from his seat outside the tent and towered over me.

I was taken aback by his height even though it made sense with the rest of his build. He looked down at me.

"I'll see you tomorrow, Josephine. Bright and early," and he winked at me.

Something passed between us in that moment. More than chemistry. Some deep, primal knowing. My soul recognized his, and I think his recognized mine. We both stood there for a second, like it was a scene in a movie. The wind picked up, blowing my hair across my face.

"I better tell the guys we're going to take it easy on filming tomorrow morning," I said, the words barely making noise.

Robert nodded and cleared his throat.

"Yeah," he said. "I'll come get you in the morning."

The corner of his mouth turned up and I felt my stomach flip-flop like a fish inside me.

I smiled at him, feeling a rush of blood to my cheeks. But there was something different about this with him. I didn't care if he saw. I felt no embarrassment and he kept looking at me, still half-smiling. Finally, I spoke.

"See you in the morning," I said.

And then I turned and went to talk to Matt.

FIVE

AFTER THE FORECAST of rain became the official word running through camp, everyone was more than happy to take the day off filming. I half-wondered if Matt wasn't a little relieved to not have to go out for a second try with the lions right away. There's no denying the encounter was intense, though I think I found it more enjoyable than he did.

For a few minutes, I felt alive. Especially when the lion charged, throwing itself on the Jeep.

As I laid in my sleeping bag, I wondered if Robert experienced moments like that frequently. It occurred to me that I hadn't asked him what other stories he'd worked on. It also occurred to me with more clarity than earlier that I didn't know this man and I was planning on going away from camp, into the brush in a foreign country with him.

"You've lost your mind," I muttered to myself, rolling

onto my back and rubbing my eyes until I saw stars. I stared up at the ceiling of the tent. Around 3:00 in the morning, the rain began. It was light at first, and continued in that fashion for a few hours. By morning, it was pouring and we were having to seek shelter in the main building on the reserve.

I'd already dressed for my expedition, unable to sleep through the night. In my khaki shorts and blouse with the sleeves rolled up, I was ready to go. Despite the fact that it was raining, Africa was still hot.

All of us sat in the main building, sharing some coffee and breakfast items. And then Robert came in, soaked from the downpour, carrying two bags which I assumed were full of camera equipment.

"Get a load of that guy," Matt whispered to me, turning to look at Robert as he made his entrance, dripping wet and a little disheveled.

I didn't say anything in return, but I watched Robert. His eyes searched the area and found me. A smile broke across his face and he walked over.

"This is Matt," I told him as he approached, standing up and introducing him to my camera operator.

Robert stuck out his hand and I could tell Matt was taken aback, unsure what time I was using to make friends on our little international trip. He eyed Robert suspiciously, even more so when I told him our plan to go out to get some photographs together.

"You aren't a photographer," Matt said simply.

"I am today," I told him, shutting the conversation down.

"Just come back in one piece, okay?" Matt said under his breath.

"Let's go," Robert said, leaning close to me. I felt his breath against my cheek. And I turned to follow him out into the rain.

"Where are we going?" I asked.

"Not far," he told me.

It should have sent a shiver down my spine. I knew better than to trust strange men. My childhood had taught me that was never a good thing to do. But there was something about Robert that brought my defenses right down.

When I looked at him—even the first time—I saw myself reflected in his eyes. We were the same. I knew in that moment that he was wounded badly, just like me. And I knew that I wanted to know him.

It was like our souls collided the first time we made eye contact, recognizing the similarities in their design, and thinking, *Oh, yes. This one.*

I'd never experienced anything like that.

There had never been a boy or a man in my past that had made me feel those things. I'd never looked at someone and fallen in love at first sight. I'm not sure that I'd ever been in love until Robert.

He took me with him, deep into the brush. We reached a certain point and he stopped the Jeep. Even though it was raining, he climbed out and I did the same.

He gestured for me to follow him and I did as I was told. We hiked at least 3 kilometers in the rain and then he crouched down, sneaking up behind some thick brush and beckoned me to join him. He held a finger over his mouth and began to get his camera from his bag as quietly as he could.

I got up beside him and then peered through the brush.

There were lions. A pride of them. Likely the male from yesterday. There were many females this time. Some of them were grooming themselves. Others played and the male sat in the middle of it, surveying his kingdom. More than likely, he was keeping watch for any sort of abnormality.

Like me and Robert.

"The poachers are just over there," Robert whispered, pointing straight ahead.

I peered through the brush again, and far in the distance, caught sight of shadowy movement behind more brush. Robert handed me a pair of binoculars.

With their assistance, everything became much clearer.

There were several men, guns slung over their shoulders, pacing around near two Jeeps. One of them lit a cigarette, taking a long drag.

"Is that them?" I asked.

When I was a little girl and I heard stories about poachers, I imagined some sort of frightful monster illegally hunting down game. I hadn't imagined ordinary men with no outstanding qualities. I felt let down. Somehow, it was worse that there was nothing extraordinary about these men.

You might have seen them anywhere and had no idea.

"That's them," Robert confirmed.

He'd gotten his camera out and set up, ready to photograph anything the poachers might do.

I watched through the binoculars, the two of us squatting in silence, waiting for them to make a move. Finally, two of the men watching the lions through the brush seemed to have decided it was time to make a move. I could see their guns poking through the brush. With the binoculars, I could see the droplets of rain on the side of one man's face as he squinted into the sight of the rifle.

I heard the shutter of Robert's camera. Fast and furious, he got several shots.

Just then, two gunshots, softened by silencers, sounding muted. But when one of the lions cried out, I knew at least one of the poachers had hit their target.

Robert pushed further into the brush to get a better look, photographing the poachers as they scared the others away while the one they'd shot was dying.

"They're coming this way," I muttered, watching the other lions retreating directly to where we were hiding.

"Get in the long grass," Robert said, pulling me into the brush with him. Together, we hid ourselves there. I watched as lion after lion paced quickly past us, all of them making noises of discontentment. The poachers approached, drawing closer to their kill and Robert got as many shots as he possibly could. "I got their faces," he said, sounding satisfied with himself.

I wasn't sure how much good that would do.

"Is poaching a big problem? For lions, I mean, specifically."

"It's gotten worse as the tiger population has drastically fallen. Lion parts are now being sold as tiger parts for medicines and spiritual purposes. The average person can't tell what kind of big cat claw or tooth they have in their hand."

"That's terrible," I said.

"Quiet," Robert hushed.

He reached out and grabbed my arm, squeezing tightly. And then he pulled me close to him.

I could hear the poachers nearing our location, speaking to each other in what I thought was Swahili, combined with some English. At least one of them was not native to Africa, seeming to need a translation for everything. It appeared that one among them was a white man from America. Despite Robert's hold on me and his urging for quiet, I couldn't help myself. I parted the grass to get a look at the American.

When I peered out of the grass, I saw a man with a distinct gut, his white shirt tucked into his standard-issue safari pants. He wore a safari hat, too, probably in an effort to keep his balding head from burning. But it was when he turned and I got a look at his face that I recognized him instantly. U. S. Senator Harlan Howard, hailing from deep East Texas and serving as a Texas senator for the last few years. And I knew he was campaigning for reelection, swearing that, unlike his opponent, he had very forward-thinking ideas about the environment.

"Get the American," I whispered to Robert.

I heard his camera shutter click a few times.

And on the fifth or sixth click, Harlan Howard looked right at us.

"Be still," Robert whispered.

My body stiffened, so close to his that I could feel the heat coming off him.

Senator Howard's eyes roved over the bush we hid in, almost like he knew someone or something was in there, watching him. Finally, the translator spoke to him.

"We must be quick, sir," he said.

Senator Howard nodded, somewhat dismissively, but ultimately made his way back to the Jeep as two of the other poachers drug the lion back to the vehicle.

I breathed a sigh of relief when they drove off.

I laughed.

"Do you realize what you just photographed?" I asked Robert.

"I'm assuming I got something good," Robert said.

"That was a U.S. Senator," I told him. "A real jackass, too. One of the points he's running for reelection on is that he cares about the environment," I added with a bitter laugh.

"Looks like we've got a story, then," Robert said.

"We?" I asked with a smile.

"I wouldn't have known who he was without you," he said. "Write up the story."

"What?"

"Write it up. We've got the pictures. And we'll get it to the press."

I stared at Robert for a second, the two of us still hiding in tall, thick prairie grass and brush. This was the opportunity I'd been looking for. This was a way out of the local news scene. This could be big, I realized.

"Are you sure?" I asked him.

He smiled at me.

"Absolutely."

We rushed back to the Jeep and with Robert's images, I crafted a press release. And then we pitched it to CNN. We heard back within thirty minutes and I wrote up the piece about Texas Senator Harlan Howard. We attached the images and my credentials as a journalist and submitted all of that to them.

Robert changed the course of my career. And the course of my life.

I slept with him that night.

It was the best sex I'd had in my entire life. That feeling that our souls recognized each other translated to intimacy. I looked into his eyes and I swore I could see little wisps of both of our souls dancing together all around us that night. I'd never felt so connected to any human being ever before.

I finished the story for the local news. But I knew that I had the opportunity for a new career if I wanted it. CNN wanted me to do a deep dive on Senator Howard. I agreed. By the time we were leaving Africa, my life was on a different trajectory than it had been when I'd arrived there.

The last night there, after everyone had gone to their tents, Robert sat down beside me at the dwindling fire in the middle of camp. He brought his phone and a Bluetooth speaker with him, plus a bottle of liquor with dubious origins. I didn't bother asking why it didn't have a label or where he'd gotten it.

We passed it back and forth, and at the end of the night, we slept together for probably the fifth time since we'd met in as many days. Matt was starting to give me the side eye in the mornings when Robert would come crawling out of my tent after I went to get coffee for both of us.

I didn't care, though. There was something special about Robert.

Both of us knew it couldn't last. It was impractical. But I felt this bond with him. And he felt it, too.

I woke up early on our last day there. I watched Robert sleeping for a little while in the dark. A sadness had come over me about leaving him behind. Finally, he woke up and caught me.

"You look sad," he said, his voice empathetic. He reached for me and pulled me close to him.

"We probably won't ever see each other again, will we?" I asked him.

"Don't say that," he said.

He kissed the top of my head.

"I don't want to let go of this," I told him.

"I don't want to, either," he said.

The two of us promised to keep in touch. I went home to Oklahoma with new possibilities lined up for me. His career advanced, too. We did keep in touch for about a year. There were tons of phone calls and lots of selfies sent between the two of us. Neither of us lost the feeling we'd had for each other when we were in Africa.

And then, things got busy. I heard from him less and less until the radio went silent one day.

SIX

I CATCH the flight to Fairbanks. There's a stop in Denver, and that layover is about an hour and a half. I walk around the Denver airport, taking in the sights with Ghost by my side. It's the middle of summer and there are families here, also on layovers, heading to places like Disney World and Disneyland. Others are going to see family in places like San Francisco, and New York City. Where I just came from.

I think about that. Going home. It's been a long time since I've done that. I've been on the run since I got Ghost.

Finally, it's time to board the plane and I head back to my gate with a couple of snacks and some reading material for the flight. I pick up a *People* magazine featuring an article about Ainsley Gold, America's Pop Princess, who has captured the zeitgeist of a generation. I figure it will be some good distracting reading from what I'm going to be thinking about once I get to Fairbanks.

The plane is packed. Which surprises me a little bit.

When I get to my row, both seats next to the window are empty and I'm glad for that. I need a little bit of time to gather my thoughts and prepare myself for what I'm going to face once I land. Ghost curls up at my feet, tucking himself as much as he can under my seat just like he's supposed to.

I know nothing about Special Agent Parker. He's new to me. And I wonder what kind of person he'll be like to work with. Calm and easy-going or uptight and resentful of my presence there? That's always a possibility with law-enforcement. Some of them seem to think I don't belong on the scene and I don't blame them for that. It's unusual for a journalist to be involved in an active crime scene, especially on the inside. It could be a liability for them.

I wonder if any of them caught me on Good Morning Today besides Parker. I'm kind of hoping it was just him.

The flight from Denver is long but easy. I eat my snacks and I read my *People* magazine, losing myself in the Ainsley Gold story for a little while. There's another crime story. Her boyfriend went missing from a yacht during a party a few years ago. He was never found, but no one was ever charged.

I take a nap and by the time I get to Fairbanks it's around seven in the evening.

There's still sunshine outside and it's not close to setting. The days are longer here in the summer than they are in the rest of the United States.

I gather my things when we land and Ghost and I head for the gate. I'm not sure what to expect when I get there, though, I know someone will be waiting for me. Likely a driver taking me to either my hotel, or to wherever the FBI is set up.

But when I emerge from baggage claim I see a man standing in a suit that can be described only as government issue. His wraparound sunglasses are still on his eyes, making him look like a Man in Black. The thought brings a smile to my face, and I wonder if he's aware of the impression he's making.

His hair is neatly cut and he has a strong jawline. He's tall but not overly so and he looks strong beneath his suit. I wonder if he's ever had to chase down a criminal on foot. The chances are he has.

I know it's him when I see him. Special Agent Lucas Parker.

There's a look about him that makes me think it would be impossible for him to be anyone else. And after I grab my bag, I walk right up to him, Ghost at my side.

As he sees me approach, a smile breaks across his face showing full teeth in a way that makes me a little uncomfortable.

"Miss Larson," he says in a bright tone, not quite fitting an FBI agent.

"How are you? I ask, holding my own with him, not wanting to be intimidated by a man.

"I'm great," he says, and shakes my hand vigorously. "I'm your ride." He says with a big smile.

"Thanks," I say.

"May I?" He gestures towards my bags. I simply nod, not wanting to be rude. He doesn't bother rolling them. Instead, he just picks it up by the handle, and then he offers to take my backpack. I turn him down, part of me wanting to keep a hold of that as some means of retaining control of the situation.

I remind myself that I probably don't need to worry about that right now. I'm so conditioned by spending my time in the company of Nathan Kelly that I feel like I should always be vying for control of the conversation or the situation. I tell myself that's not the case right now. But it's hard to believe. And there's something about Parker that strikes me as unusual.

Usually FBI agents aren't so outgoing. Or at least when they are it's because they're being aggressive. He's not aggressive, though. He just seems happy to be doing what he's doing, from what I can tell.

After I find somewhere for Ghost to relieve himself, Parker walks us to the car that's parked right in front of the double doors. A standard black sedan, the kind that you imagine FBI agents might drive. He puts my bag in the trunk and then he comes around to open the door for me. It surprises me.

"Oh," I say. "Thank you."

"Of course."

He takes Ghost's leash, with my permission, and situates him in the back seat.

Parker goes around to the driver side quickly and gets in. And just like that we're off, merging into evening traffic in Alaska.

"I would ask what brings you here," he says. "But I have a pretty good idea." He smiles.

"That you do." I say.

There's an intensity about Parker that I wasn't expecting. An intensity to his happiness that I'm not sure I've ever seen in anyone else. I wonder if it's bravado.

"I read your book," he says. "It was good."

"Thank you," I say.

Parker goes on.

"You did a good job," he says. He glances over at me in the passenger seat as he drives. "Your personal connection to Kelly was very compelling."

I don't say anything else. He goes on.

"It was really good. I think out of everybody on the planet you probably know more about Nathan Kelly than anyone," he says.

"It's a dubious honor at best," I tell him.

"I thought I'd take you by police headquarters where everyone is set up," he says. "Let you get the lay of the land."

I tell him that sounds good, and we drive on in silence for a few moments, but Parker doesn't seem to like the quiet. He seizes the opportunity to ask me some more questions.

"I read the article that CNN did about you," he offers. "It was really good."

"Thanks. It was a pretty big honor to be interviewed by them."

"You're a pretty fascinating person, you know?" Parker says.

I glance over at him.

"I wouldn't think so," I say with a laugh. "I interviewed a serial killer. That's pretty much all there is to me." I'm still looking at him and he turns. His eyes are brown and warm and his smile touches them.

"Oh, there's more to everyone."

The way he says it puts me on guard again. The smile seems genuine. But there's an intensity to it that I'm not expecting. Like he's really trying to get to know me right now, and I don't understand why. It's not something I've ever experienced with any of the law-enforcement I've worked with, the only reason I can think of is that he doesn't trust me.

It's not long before we pull up outside of the police station. It's in the downtown area of Fairbanks. Bigger than I thought it would be. Fairbanks has turned out to be a bigger city than I realized it was. Lots of population and room for someone to operate without being caught for quite some time.

It happens all the time, I remind myself. It doesn't matter where you are.

We get out of the car and Parker shows Ghost and I the way inside. It's just like any other police station and we go into the back. Uniformed officers look up from their desks, detectives do the same but they're wearing suits. Not looking too unlike Parker himself.

They all have one thing in common: the way they're looking at us.

I have an idea that all of them know who I am. They wouldn't be looking at me this way if they didn't. And even if they don't know who I am exactly, they know that I'm with Parker. And it's obvious that they know why he's here.

I offer a pressed smile to one of the officers that looks at me as we head into the back. He gives it back to me, but there's a look on his face that tells me he has some hesitancy. I guess everyone knows that someone made the decision to bring a journalist in.

I don't imagine that's something they've ever done before. It's not common practice. Most cops don't want a journalistic investigation going on within their own criminal investigation.

But the work I do is a little bit different.

And I'm not here for a story. I'm here because I've been asked to be here as the person who knows the most about Nathan Kelly out of anyone in the whole world, as Parker said.

I'm not sure how useful I'll be as we pass through two double doors and enter the hallway. Back here there are interrogation rooms. One of them seems to be in use.

The door is closed and I can hear voices on the other side.

I wonder if they've got someone in there that they think might be their guy.

And as if Parker is reading my mind, he speaks up.

"Different crime," he says. "That would be way too easy." He adds this with a smile.

I look at him, a little shocked by his words, and how in tune he is with my thoughts.

Parker leads me into a large conference room that's bustling with people. There are officers back here and detectives, and a few other men in suits that are standing around a dry erase board that has a map of Fairbanks on it.

"Well," Parker says. "This is it. Headquarters."

Despite the fact that there's a large group of people back here, there aren't a ton of papers spread over each table and the map is bare.

"When did you guys get here?" I ask.

"Only this morning," Parker says. "There's still a lot to do."

That's an understatement to say the least, I realize.

"What made you send people up here?" And by you, I mean the FBI.

He catches the drift of my question.

"Well," he says. "The girl that came out of the woods today wasn't the first. Like I told you, each of them had a zip tie around one wrist. Her and the girl that was found beside the road. It turns out, the girl who escaped isn't from Alaska. She's from California. There's a suspicion of a Kelly copycat serial killer as well as a crime that's crossed state lines."

"Has anyone talked to her?" I ask.

"The girl that came out of the woods? No. She's in the hospital, in a medically induced coma. As soon as— and *if*—she's well enough, we're going to go talk to her."

It's sparse, but it's a start, I realize. I think people would be horrified to know how little the cops have to go on sometimes in cases like these. Especially in the beginning.

"Let me introduce you," Parker says. I nod and he leads me to the front of the room. I feel like I'm being introduced to professors. And I'm the new student, the men at the front are gathered in a group talking amongst themselves, completely unaware of our presence as we approach. Or at least they seem that way.

"Gentlemen," Parker says as he clears his throat.

The men standing together turn to us. One of them is balding, older, and very serious looking. I assume that he's the one in charge, and when he speaks, I'm not wrong.

"You're the journalist," the bald man says. There's a note of irritation in his voice. I can tell that he doesn't really want me to be here. I know better than to explain myself, aware that if I start to, it will only turn into a confrontation.

"I am," I say.

He looks at me, clearly expecting me to put up more

of a fight than that. To have reacted to the tone in his question.

I stick out my hand to shake his, and he stands there for a moment looking at it, hesitating. Or maybe making me wait, and trying to put me off kilter. I just stare at him, a smile on my face and my hand outstretched. I don't move. If he's not going to shake my hand, I'm going to make him tell me that.

He narrows his eyes slightly. He doesn't like that I've backed him into a corner like this.

Finally, he reaches out his hand and shakes mine.

"Nice to meet you," I say, mustering up all the genuine emotion that I can. "Josephine Larson," I add, giving him my name.

My dad taught me to always be polite. And that people don't remember much about you other than how you make them feel. And I want this man to know that I belong here. That I've been asked to be here. And he's not going to intimidate me out of doing my job.

"Special Agent Wilson," the balding man says. He tilts his head back, as if he's sizing me up. "You came highly recommended," he adds. "Don't disappoint me."

He holds on to my hand as he says the last. It's a direct threat, though I'm not sure how much bite there is to it. I don't answer to him outside of the capacity I'm acting in right now. But he does have the ability to take me off the case.

"I wouldn't think of it," I say with a smile before he

lets go of my hand. "If you don't mind me asking," I add. "Who recommended me?"

Wilson turns his eyes to Parker.

"Special Agent Parker did."

He says it with a level of disgust I wasn't expecting.

My eyes widen and I turn to Parker, looking at him like I'm seeing him for the first time.

Lucas Parker resists making eye contact with me.

I wasn't expecting that, either.

SEVEN

"WHY DON'T we go get something to eat?" Special Agent Parker says, breaking the tension.

I nod, being agreeable. Anything to get out from under Wilson's eye. His stare is heavy, and I can tell he meant what he said about being disappointed. He doesn't want me here.

I don't blame him. There's nothing conventional about this. And he strikes me as the kind of guy that's done everything by the book the entire time he's worked at the FBI. I notice him looking at Ghost with disdain. I already don't like this guy, though Ghost seems unaware of his disapproval. Wilson seems easy to read.

Parker on the other hand seems like he might be a wild card.

I wasn't expecting him to have been the one to recommend me. The way he asked questions in the car made me think he might have even been skeptical of bringing me on. I wonder now if it was just genuine interest.

Parker leads us out of the conference room, back into the hallway, and we head out through the front of the police station.

"I didn't realize you had recommended me," I say as we head out onto the sidewalk towards the car.

"I'm full of surprises," Parker says.

"That you are," I say.

Parker opens the door for me again, a gentlemanly move. He lets Ghost into the back again.

I get into the car and I buckle my seatbelt. He walks around to the other side of the car and gets in the driver seat doing the same. The sun is starting to set in Fairbanks. It's close to 9:30 at night, I'm starting to get hungry, and I wouldn't turn down a shower.

"Is it all right if we run by the hotel really quick?" I ask. "I think I want to take a shower."

"That's totally fine with me," Parker says. "I could use a shower, too."

It makes me laugh like a kid. He catches it.

"Not like that," he says with a laugh. "You haven't even bought me dinner yet."

I look over at him, smirk on my face. I'm used to men trying to put me off my game by making inappropriate comments. Parker seems different, though.

Even in the dim lights of the police station I can see that Parker is blushing. The thought makes me want to laugh all over again.

It's not often that men experience that at the hands of women. Particularly in male-dominated fields like this. I've come across so many guys that did their best to make me uncomfortable with offhanded sexual remarks. Parker seems like a nice guy, but I don't feel guilty in the slightest.

"I knew what you meant," I say. I decide to put him out of his misery, squirming in the front seat as we back out of the parking lot parking space.

He doesn't say anything. I make a mental note to not bring up the fact that both of us are going to shower when we get to the hotel.

I try to think of something to say to fill the silence, and then the obvious comes to me.

"Why did you recommend me?" I ask.

"I read your book," he says simply. He goes on. "It was phenomenal. The research you did was meticulous. The amount of information that you got out of Nathan Kelly was astonishing. How are you able to do that?" He glances over at me now, apparently over the shower comment.

"I think he didn't see me as a threat," I say. "He thinks so little of women I don't think he could fathom me being able to get the upper hand on him."

"You have a calming presence about you," Parker says. It's not the observation I was expecting from him. "I could see how Kelly would be comfortable talking to you."

We drive through the streets of Fairbanks and we

pass down a street with all the bars you could ask for. People are walking in and out, the streets are busy. It's a Friday night. And everyone is carrying on like there's not a serial killer walking amongst them.

"What was it like interviewing him?" Parker asks me.

"It was interesting," I say. "He had the blackest eyes of anyone I've ever met." I surprise myself by saying that. It's not an observation I put in my book. But a personal one that affected me. There was something about Nathan Kelly's eyes that contained infinite darkness. It was like all the evil in his soul had collected there in a vast pool that could suck you in at a moment's notice. "Sometimes he was hard to interview," I admit, changing gears. "You'd ask him a question and he'd dance around the answer, enjoying the fact that he was getting to spend time out of his cell. I think any prisoner is grateful for a break in the monotony, and Kelly was no different. I gave him Dr. Pepper, candy bars, and cigarettes. That's what he'd ask for. And as long as he had those, he kept talking. He loved the sound of his own voice," I say, and then I'm quiet for a moment.

"I think most of them do," Parker says.

"He got off on rehashing it, reliving it."

"The worst is when you have to take them back to the scene of the crime. When you're trying to get some bit of information about where someone's buried, or where we might find the remains. Watching their eyes glaze over as they describe the murder is awful. It feels like you're giving them pleasure by allowing them to do it. But you have no choice," Parker says. "It's like making a deal with the devil."

"That's exactly what it was like," I say. "But I can't imagine what it would be like in your position. In a situation like that."

"You get used to it," Parker says. "It becomes part of the job."

"How do you shut it off?" I ask. And I realize as soon as the question is out of my mouth I'm not just asking to fill the silence. I'm asking because I want to know.

"Shut off what?" Parker asks. He glances over at me as he steers, driving down the road.

"Do you find yourself thinking about it afterwards? Like when you lay in bed at night? Or sometimes in the middle of dinner with your friends?" I ask. My voice is meek, vulnerable. I look out the window, and instead of the streets of Fairbanks, but for a split second, I'm back in the woods, thirteen years old, holding on to my friend Jordan's arm for dear life.

"It can be hard," Parker says. "Guys don't talk about it very much. It's not something we really get into at work, how we process all this after we clock out."

We ride the rest of the way to the hotel in silence, and soon he's turning into a parking garage next to a big brand-name hotel in downtown Fairbanks.

I grab my bag out of the back and let Ghost out, and together we head into the hotel. Seemingly the gentleman, Parker waits with me at the front desk while I get my arrangements made. They reserved a hotel room for me and it's only a few minutes before I have the key in hand and we're headed up to the eighth floor together. Apparently this is where they're housing all the agents and people associated with the case.

We say nothing to each other in the elevator and once we get off, we both turn the same way headed for our respective rooms. Mine comes up first and I stop. Parker keeps on walking without saying anything. I glance down the hall, watching him as he finally finds his room. He holds his key up to the door. I hear the beep and the sound of the lock unengaging as he opens it. Just before he steps in, he looks back at me.

"I can be done in about 15 minutes," he says. "I'll wait for you down at the bar."

"See you there," I say.

Part of me wants to tell him that he doesn't have to wait for me at the bar. That I'm a grown woman and I can find food for myself tonight. Ghost will be with me. That I'd be just as happy ordering room service, regardless of the quality of it. I have little desire to go out into the night and find a diner. Ghost and I are both ready to rest.

I go inside and lock the door behind me. I let Ghost off his leash and I wheel my suitcase over to the closet and prop it up on the little luggage rack. Opening it, I get my toiletries out. I make short work of the shower, feeling like I need to hurry since he'll probably be waiting for me. It's irritating. I just wanna have a moment to myself. I haven't gotten one of those all day.

I towel dry my hair and hit it with the blow dryer.

The natural waves come out and I'm fine with that. I'm not worried about winning any beauty contest out here.

Finally, after I'm dressed in fresh clothes and I've brushed my teeth and washed my face, I take Ghost for a little potty break and then go back upstairs. I head down the hallway where I half expect to see Parker waiting on me. But he's not there.

I go back to the elevator and make my way down to the lobby. When I get out, I look to my left and spot the bar. I see Special Agent Lucas Parker already having a drink, waiting patiently for me and Ghost.

I walk over and Parker sees me. He gives me a nod and a smile.

"There she is," he says, seemingly excited to see me. I wonder if he's already had more than one.

"Look," I say. "I apologize for getting all philosophical earlier, and—"

"No, I apologize," he says seriously, putting down his drink that appears to be whiskey. "Men should be more open with their feelings," he says with a smile, and for a moment I wonder if he's being sarcastic. But he's not. "It's a hard job. I've seen some awful shit. Heard even worse shit. And it's hard not to carry it around with you. So I can't even imagine what it would be like to carry these things I know around with me if I were a woman."

His face turns serious at the last.

"It can be incredibly hard," I admit softly.

"How about a drink?" he offers. "It's on me. Or rather, on the Bureau," he says with a smile.

"Can't turn down a drink on Hoover's dime," I say teasingly. The mood has lightened.

Maybe it's a result of the alcohol, or maybe Parker thinks I'm someone he can trust. Either way, I'm grateful for it. And the alcohol does a little to put my nerves at ease, banishing my visions of campgrounds. Or so I hope.

"What do you say we get something to eat?" Parker asks. His energy is high.

"I'd be game for that," I say. "I'm starving." I don't bother telling him that as my father used to say, I could eat the asshole out of an armadillo.

It was one of the many colorful phrases he used around me when I was growing up. Phrases not suitable for a little girl to repeat at school. I got in trouble in kindergarten once for using a Pete Larson special. My mom was furious. My dad thought it was hilarious.

Parker downs his drink, and I do the same, finishing my whiskey off like it's a shot. My chest burns and I contort my face at the taste of it. He laughs when he sees me do that.

We head out into the night, walking down the street.

"There's a little diner right up here," Parker says. "I've been eating there a lot since I've been here. Probably not the best place for health food, but it's certainly a comfort in these trying times."

Parker does strike me as someone who takes care of his health. He's in great shape. Now that I've seen him without his jacket on, it's obvious that he's very muscular. And it doesn't look like the kind of muscular that only belongs in a gym. His body looks functional. Like he can run fast, far and hard. Like he could restrain anyone he needed to at any given point. Yet he still has a slenderness about him that makes him seem wiry and athletic. I wouldn't mind having him in my corner if the moment came to that.

He looks a lot different than Rob.

The thought dumps over me like ice water. I hadn't planned to think something like that. But thoughts of Rob are often, unexpected, and punch me in the gut at the worst time. I tell myself he's only on my mind today because I saw that Facebook post.

I guess he's doing well for himself, working for NatGeo and getting his photographs featured on their Facebook page. I wonder if they've made the magazine. The war in Ukraine is such a hot topic right now, I can't imagine how he wouldn't have been featured in some article.

Parker and I walk down the sidewalk, and as we make our way to the bustling part of downtown, the street gets busier. Finally, we find ourselves at the diner that Parker has claimed as his home away from home. Edna's is the name. A neon sign declares that proudly in hot pink. Inside the floor is lined with black-and-white checkerboard tiles. The booths are also pink and vinyl, not to mention sparkly. There's even a bar with barstools that match the vinyl booths. It looks like an old-timey diner. A blast from the past. Parker opens the door for me and gestures for me to go ahead.

"Ladies first," he says with a smile.

It's contagious. But it's not lost on me that even though we're having a good time tonight, the reality is that I'm here to help with a murder investigation.

Somehow that seems wrong. That we could be having fun right now while there are women being abducted from campgrounds. It's so strange. Exactly how Nathan Kelly would get his victims. I can certainly imagine how the conclusion has been drawn that these crimes have something to do with Kelly's.

We find a booth and sit down, grabbing sticky menus from behind the mustard and ketchup bottles. The place is the definition of an anachronistic greasy spoon. There's something about it that's very comforting. It reminds me of the diner my dad and I used to go to on Saturday mornings.

On the weekends, he would do handyman jobs and he would take me with him. He put me to work doing this or that, things that seemed important at the time but I'm not really sure they were. He made me feel important. I'd hand him his tools and he'd get to work. I observed everything he did. Every Saturday morning we would go to the same diner before things got started. This place reminds me of it.

The thought is bittersweet, a nice memory with an edge to it.

Parker orders a cheeseburger with fries and I get a club sandwich. My standard when I go anywhere that I'm not familiar with. No one makes a bad club sandwich. And my theory proves right when they serve it. I take a bite and it's one of the best I've ever had.

Maybe that's just the jet lag talking. But it seems awfully damn good.

"Tell me about you," I venture after wiping a bit of mayonnaise off the corner of my mouth. I take a gulp of water and swallow down my food.

Parker is in the middle of chewing a bite of his cheeseburger. He holds up a finger, indicating that I need to give him a minute. I nod, but continue watching him. He swallows and takes a drink, then smiles at me.

"You certainly don't mince words, Miss Larson," he says with that same disarming smile he wore earlier. "I don't know what there is to tell," he says, pushing his finished plate to the side and leaning in on his elbows.

"You asked me why I was interested in this sort of thing," I say. "Why do you do this kind of work?"

"What? Track down bad guys?" he asks, still leaning forward as he says it. There's an intensity to his gaze, like he's debating what he might say next. Like there's a standard answer he gives most people, but he's thinking about telling me the truth.

"Yeah," I say, not letting on that I find anything about his posture intense.

Something passes over his features, and it's gone just as quickly. I recognize it. I know that darkness.

Just then, my phone vibrates in my pocket. I ignore it, first thinking it's a text. But it continues.

"Sorry," I say, pulling my phone out and placing it on

the table. I'm about to reject the call when I notice the number.

It starts with 1-800.

A collect call.

No way.

"Take it," Parker says with a smile.

I just nod and stand from the booth. I take Ghost's leash as I hurry out onto the sidewalk and slide my finger across the screen to answer the call.

A robotic voice speaks first. And then it's followed by a very familiar voice as it pipes through the connection, right into my ear. A voice that I haven't heard in a long time. Over a year. But I'd know it anywhere.

Someone bumps my shoulder on the sidewalk, telling me to watch out. I don't move.

"You have a collect call from," the robotic voice says. And then he speaks. "Nathan Kelly."

EIGHT

"YES," I say, accepting the call. Immediately I'm connected to the man I spent the previous three years interviewing.

"Hello, Josephine," Nathan says.

His voice is like vermin, crawling over my body with scabby little feet, damp from the sewer in which they reside. Normally, I would have several hours to prepare myself for it when I drove down to see him. Phone calls were done on my terms during the course of our working relationship.

"Hello, Nathan," I say into the receiver.

A car honks and startles me. I jump slightly and then tuck myself out of the way into a little alcove next to the diner door.

"I'm sure you've seen the news," he says. Nathan Kelly has a silky, southern accent. It gives me the creeps.

It's the kind of accent though that women would find attractive if they met him in some other way than being kidnapped by him. It's a voice that I hear in my nightmares.

And now in my waking reality.

It's something that I thought I left behind, far in the past, with the writing of the book. I had intended to extend my relationship with Kelly no longer than I had to. Anything longer than what was professionally necessary would be bad for anyone's mental health.

"I have," I say. I watch the people as they walk back-and-forth in front of me, traveling to the diner, or a bar down the road, or maybe to some other location. They all passed me without the knowledge that the man I'm talking to on the phone is the most gruesome serial killer that the United States has ever seen. He makes all the big names look like amateurs. It's a dubious honor at best.

"You see what they're sayin'?" he asks, as if we're having some innocuous conversation that has nothing to do with the murder of an innocent woman. Or perhaps women at this point. And there's a note in his voice that I really dislike. He's excited by this, quickened by the thought that he might be in the news again.

"What are they saying, Nathan?" I ask, doing my best to play dumb.

"You know I saw you on TV this morning," he says. "I guess you could say that I made you famous."

"My intention was never to get famous," I say with

finality, trying to indicate that the discussion about any fame I might've gained from writing about him is over. But Nathan Kelly isn't a person that abides by boundaries.

"You could've fooled me," he says. His tone is that of someone having an easy-going conversation. It puts me right back there in the room in front of him. That was his modus operandi, to talk about these things like it was no big deal. The shift would occur when he talked about the murders in detail, his dark eyes would get darker pupils dilating with pleasure and memory. He talked about the murders like they were something holy. A sacrifice that he'd been asked to make by God himself.

When I was conducting my interviews with Kelly, he would speak about the murders that way, calling them his work. Like it was art. A portfolio of his most recent designs, all of them divinely inspired. And I guess in a way he was exercising an artistic impulse, he carved out a letter to a local news anchor that he thought was pretty on the back of one of the women that he killed addressing her by name.

That never made the news.

He told me he'll always be bitter about that. That if anything about the entire case should've made the news, that was it.

He told me how he did it. Laying the woman out on his coffee table and scraping at her back with a dental tool that he bought at Walgreens. He carved until he wore away the first few layers of flesh. The message had looked like hot pink neon, he told me. I glance up at the sign over Edna's and can't help but notice the similarities between that and the crime scene photo I was ultimately shown of the incident. He wasn't wrong.

"What can I do for you tonight?" I finally ask him.

He seems to think about this. And then he speaks.

"You really think that old boy in Alaska was inspired by me?"

The question is chilling, because the way he says it, he sounds like an aspiring artist being struck by his influence. Like this is one of the most humbling experiences he could have in his position, like for him the true horror lies in people forgetting what he contributed to the world, no matter how gruesome or dark. "I don't know," I say.

It's the truth. At this point, I don't know.

"I bet you're up in Alaska right now," he says with certainty. He talks to me like he might talk to an old friend.

Maybe I am the closest thing that Nathan Kelly's got to a friend.

"Why would you think that?" I ask.

"Because I know you, Joey."

I'm shocked into silence. The nickname is one that only one person uses with me. My father. And I haven't heard it in a long time.

"You don't," I say firmly. "I have to go."

Before he can speak, I hang up the phone and stand

there on the street with it shaking in my hand. I stare at it for a moment as if it might bite me. As if he might call back at any second. I jump when someone almost bumps into me, part of me being scared that the person might've been him right here in Fairbanks. It makes me wonder if he's watching me somehow. The thought that he could know that about me because he thinks he knows me so well is disgusting. It's vile. And I refuse to accept that. Nathan Kelly does not know me. He knows what I let him know about me. And everything I've let him know about me I've used to my advantage.

"Everything all right?" I hear Parker's voice and I spin.

"Fine," I say. And then I realize I should probably tell him who I was just talking to. It's the whole reason he brought me out here, my connection with Nathan Kelly. "Guess who I just talked to."

Parker shakes his head like he wouldn't know who to guess.

"Kelly."

His eyes widen. He jerks his head back in shock.

"That was quick," he says.

"You expected him to call me?"

"I'd be lying if I said no," Parker says. "I had a feeling he might. Not so soon, though." He furrows his brow "What did he say?"

"Not much of value," I tell him. "Mostly I think he was calling to brag. I think he finds it exhilarating that the connection is being made in the media between this guy here in Alaska and Kelly himself. He mentioned something about fame. My fame from writing a book about him. But I think it was really about his fame. He wanted to remind me that he was someone."

Parker shakes his head and puts his hands on his hips.

"I'm really shocked he called this soon," Parker says.

"I hadn't heard from him in a long time," I say. "But I had a gut feeling if I was going to hear from him anytime it was going to be right now. He wouldn't miss an opportunity like this to relive his crimes."

Parker nods.

"I think we should probably get back to the station," he says. "Maybe you could write up a little report of what he told you in the phone call. I know it wasn't much, but we might need it."

I nod at Parker, understanding the significance of the phone call.

He leads the way back to the car in the parking garage at the hotel. We get inside and head back to the police station. We don't say much on the drive, and I'm rolling over the conversation with Kelly in my mind. I keep coming back to the idea that he's watching me. It was something that I had to talk myself out of in the early days of interviewing him. He had this way of speaking to you that made you think he was watching every move. It was unnerving. I realized pretty early on that it was something he did to maintain control of people. There was a highway in the prison, and Kelly was smart enough to take advantage of that. He would use his knowledge to get favors from people, even prison guards.

I can still remember looking up from the table where I was sitting across from Nathan Kelly, and realizing that the guard had left us completely alone.

I shake my head as we drive, trying to shake off the memory and sensation that Nathan Kelly's being is crawling all over my body.

His energy lingers on my skin like an unwanted touch. Even through the phone, he has this effect. It reminds me of all the time I spent interviewing him. The hour long scalding showers I'd take when I got back to my hotel after spending a day with him. I'd scrub my skin and let the water run over it until it was raw and red. The heat radiated off of it even when I crawled between the cool, clean sheets. I spent so many nights wondering what it would be like to *not* be able to escape Nathan Kelly's presence. His *physical* presence.

The way it was for the women that disappeared from those campgrounds without a trace.

I'd be lying if I said there weren't times that the interviews got to me. My only job, besides taking down the information in detail, at that time was not to let him rattle me. Rather, not to let him become aware that he *had* rattled me. Because he managed to a lot.

I can still see him rolling a new cigarette across his knuckles, weaving in front of and behind each one. His fingers were slender and flexible enough that he never so much as put a dent in the paper of the cigarette, even after doing this for a solid twenty minutes. I learned that he did this when he was close to revealing something he wasn't sure he wanted to quite yet. Something that excited him. Usually something absolutely horrific.

When I was on the phone with him just now, I imagined him doing that. Rolling that fresh cigarette across his knuckles, taunting me because he knew something.

It's a virtual impossibility that he could know anything, isn't it?

I don't want to go down that path.

A woman came out of the woods this morning, and there's no solid proof yet linking him to any of this. It's theory at best. Probably the FBI and the cops hoping they'll get lucky with this one. A copycat that follows Nathan Kelly's every move. It would make their job easier.

Otherwise, they're back at square one.

It's a lot easier to assume that this is halfway in the bag. At least this way, they kind of have an idea of who they're looking for. Or so they think.

That's one of the things about Nathan Kelly. He looks like he could be anyone.

There's nothing particularly remarkable about him. He's not unattractive, but neither is he disarmingly handsome. He's of average height. Average build. He would fit in in a crowd of any kind.

He's a chameleon.

And that's his strength.

Which is probably this guy's strength, too.

He could be anyone.

Parker pulls us up in front of the police station again. It's close to 10:00pm at this point. Part of me just longs for the privacy of my hotel room again. I'm exhausted and jet lagged and ready to call it a day. But Parker is ready to go. He gives me the impression that he never sleeps.

"Here we are again," he says with a smile.

Even though his words and his attitude are good-natured, there's something intense behind it. Like at any moment, he could turn into someone else. Someone that I haven't met yet.

He looks up at me as he unbuckles his seatbelt.

"Let's go," he says with a firm encouragement for me to go ahead and get out of the car.

I force a smile back and bite down any urge I might have had to tell him that I'd really just like to go back to my hotel room. That's not an option. At least not yet.

I shut the door behind myself, then get Ghost out of the back. Parker opens the door leading into the police station for me. He follows closely behind and we're met with a gust of cool air inside.

He leads the way back to the conference room that's functioning like a war room for the present time. When we enter, there are more markings on the map. More things have been hung up with magnets on the dry erase board. It looks like while we've been gone, someone has gone through what evidence they have to start piecing things together.

I spot Wilson at the front, arms folded in a folding chair, feet kicked up on the table in front of him. He's listening to two men in polo shirts, both of them wearing a weapon on their hip. One is talking animatedly while the other seems to be gauging Wilson's response. But his face is a stony mask, not easily penetrated by whatever theory the younger guy is pitching at him.

By the time we get up there, the two men in polo shirts with guns have left to continue on their work and Wilson is staring at the dry erase board with his hands behind his head. He spots Special Agent Parker without even looking at him. In the periphery of his vision, he's seen us approach.

"Parker," he says instead of *hello*. "And Miss Larson."

"Josephine," I insist.

"Josephine," he corrects himself and turns to face us, kicking his feet off the table. He brings his elbows to rest on his knees. "Have a seat." He stares at Ghost.

I glance at Parker quickly, feeling like Wilson's about to tell us something important.

"I want all the notes you have from when you were writing your book about Kelly," Wilson says, looking directly at me. "Are they digital? Physical?"

"Everything's digital. Things I wrote on notebook paper have been scanned. I have it all in the Cloud."

"Perfect," Wilson says. "I want it all on this table," he gestures next to him. "By tomorrow morning."

"No problem," I say.

"And you help her," he says to Parker.

There's a note of resentment in his tone.

Parker sighs ever so slightly. If I weren't listening for it, I wouldn't hear it.

"Yes, sir," Parker says without making eye contact with either of us.

I get the distinct impression that this is some kind of shit work for him, and that even though he's the one that suggested bringing me in, he hadn't planned on babysitting me the whole time.

"We've got another body!" An officer shouts over the conversations being held all around us. "Same area as the last one. Naked female."

I spin to look at the cop giving the news.

Immediately FBI agents head for the double doors of the conference room.

"Think you can handle going to the scene?" Wilson asks me.

I spin to face him. I've seen crime scene photos before. The most gruesome kind, even. Still, I'm not sure I'm prepared for the real thing. But I have to make a decision in a split second. I glance at Parker. He presses his lips together and glances at Wilson. Something passes between them. An unspoken exchange giving me the idea that neither of them think I'm big enough to handle being at a real crime scene.

"Of course," I say, irritated by the thought. "I grew up in a trailer park. I've seen some pretty gnarly stuff," I try to tease, lightening the moment. But neither of them seem to think I'm funny. And of course, it's not funny. It's nerves.

"Go," Wilson says to the pair of us. And when we don't both jump up immediately, he reiterates it. "Go!" He waves his arms at us.

I stand, and so does Parker. He looks at me and gestures toward the double doors.

"Shall we?"

NINE

PARKER DRIVES and we follow the series of cop cars and unmarked vehicles that are headed for the highway. There's an urgency. Everyone's going over the speed limit and following a bare minimum of traffic laws. I don't blame them. Everyone in Fairbanks and the surrounding areas are on edge tonight.

I can't imagine what it's like at a campground right now.

Barren, I think.

But the thought occurs to me that there might be someone there who hasn't heard the news. A free spirit who's traveled all the way up from California on a journey to find herself. Only to end up in an empty campground with a serial killer setting his sights on her.

The thought is enough to turn my stomach. I'm overcome with an uneasiness.

Parker and I don't talk all the way there. We drive for

what seems like forever, but it's no more than thirty or forty-five minutes.

Finally, everyone starts pulling off onto the shoulder of the highway. There's a steep hill on the right side, terminating in a level piece of ground that might be fifty yards wide. And that's where everyone is gathered.

I see flashing blue and red lights. An ambulance with EMTs that aren't moving quickly. Or at all. There's a black van with the back doors open parked close by. Someone has a massive light positioned in the level part of the grass and people are gathered around. There are more searching with flashlights walking in every direction around the congregation of people.

Parker parks the car and we get out. I leave Ghost in the car. As we approach, I'm hit with a foul odor.

Not that of decomposition, but that of someone living in squalor, covered in their own filth. That and the iron scent of blood. The odor is so strong that I pull my shirt up over my nose as we approach the lighted area.

"You should probably get a look," Parker says as I hesitate to part the crowd to get closer. "Your opinion is the whole reason you're here," he reminds me.

I don't take my eyes off the people in front of me, imagining that there's a dead woman only a few feet in front of all of us.

Parker parts the crowd and pulls me through by my hand. His palm is warm, a reminder of life in the midst of death. And finally, we emerge near the body and I take it in.

The woman laying in the grass is contorted, her limp body obviously dumped with such carelessness that her limbs are bent at odd angles. Her skin is yellowed and bruised everywhere, and there are severe lacerations on her thighs, stomach, and arms that show signs of the abuse she suffered prior to her death.

Two fingernails on her right hand have been ripped out, presumably while she was fighting the person that killed her.

Her hair is thin, making me think whoever had her kept her for some time didn't take care of her in any way. She's incredibly skinny, with her joints standing out like steel balls covered by skin stretched too tight over them. Her face is gaunt and her eyes are open, her eyeballs sunken into her head and more than beginning to be dried out.

It's readily apparent that a bird has been eating one of them today.

There's a bullet hole in her forehead. Right in the middle. A clean shot. I see no others. That's what killed her.

She was shot like game.

Just like Nathan Kelly would shoot his victims.

And the lacerations are just like those found on his victims who he would use for target practice at his cabin. He'd get drunk, tie them spread eagle against the wall with hooks he'd installed for such a purpose. Then he'd throw knives at the women. Not to kill them, just to terrorize them.

He could smell their fear. He told me that was his favorite part.

And right now, I'm smelling the rotten remains of that sensory experience.

I turn and step out of the crowd, running for the edge of the road, trying to get as far away as I can to keep from contaminating the scene.

And then I throw up my dinner.

I'm swiping at the corners of my mouth and wiping away tears when Parker gets to me. He places a hand on my back in an unexpected gesture of kindness.

"You alright?" He asks.

"I'm fine," I assure him. "The smell."

"Yeah, the smell is a lot," he agrees. "She must have been left in her own feces while he held her captive."

It's what Nathan Kelly would do.

He reduced those women to animals before he hunted them. It's the same modus operandi. He wanted them as weak as possible, hardly an indication of a fair fight.

But he wasn't interested in fair.

He wanted to terrorize them.

That was the end game.

And judging by the way this poor young woman lying in the ditch looks, I'd say whoever did this had the same goal in mind.

"We need to talk to the woman that made it out of the woods," I tell Parker.

He nods.

"She's been in the hospital ever since. We're waiting for the go ahead, but I can make a few calls and see if we can get in to see her soon. I'll see how she's doing."

"Do that," I say. "Please." I add just in case I sound bossy, and I immediately regret it. He asked me here for my expertise, not my politeness. Every woman's found herself in that position, either apologizing or kneecapping a request even though they're the one that's supposed to be calling some of the shots.

Not that I'm entirely in charge. It's a tightrope you walk as a woman. Never be too blunt. Always say you're sorry, even if you don't need to. Never be rude. They'll think you're a bitch. And don't be too bossy if you're in a position with any semblance of power. That gets you labeled worse names than a bitch.

But Parker doesn't hesitate. He simply nods and excuses himself, getting his phone out of his pocket. He steps out of earshot and makes his call.

I glance back at the crime scene. The bright light still shines down on the woman's body. And it's then that I see Crime Scene Investigators starting to bag things up and collect evidence. All the bags are small, and I wonder what they've found around her. Probably personal belongings. Things that were dumped with her body. But I'm certain something is missing.

There's no way this guy didn't want a momento. A trophy, in criminological terms.

I walk back over and brave the scene again. The smell is still rank and powerful, but I manage this time. I look down at her thin frame and direct my eyes to her neck. No necklace. When I look at her wrists and fingers, I see no jewelry there. But I do see a neon yellow zip tie.

The same color that Kelly would use. The color was a detail that never made it to the press. It sends a chill through me.

She's seemingly lost enough weight—and it's been long enough—that there are no indentations on her fingers of where a ring might have been.

The Crime Scene Investigators mumble amongst themselves as they collect evidence and take photographs of the scene. They're meticulous, and I hope they miss nothing.

The agent next to me turns to size me up when he realizes he doesn't know who I am and I'm standing beside him.

I seize the opportunity to introduce myself.

"Josephine Larson," I say, sticking my hand out while a dead body rests just a few feet in front of us.

"Special Agent Andrew Harris," the man says in return. He gives my hand a firm shake, but he offers me the slightest smile as he does so. I offer it back. "Parker brought you in," he says, and I confirm his thought with a nod. "So, you wrote the book on Nathan Kelly?" he asks. Then he adds, "Literally."

"I guess you could say that," I reply. "Literally."

"I read the book," he admits. "I wanted to see how wrong you were about the whole thing." He sticks his jaw out with a smirk. "But you got it pretty damn near perfect."

"That's what happens when you spend a year living in a hotel next to a prison so you can interview a serial killer day after day," I say with a modest laugh.

"What the hell made you want to do that?" Special Agent Harris asks.

My memory lapses into a scene. Jordan and I running through the trees the night her mother was abducted.

I snap myself out of the memory.

"I've just always been interested in that sort of thing," I tell him with a shrug, hoping he'll change the subject. But with a dead body lying a few feet from us that might have been the victim of a serial killer acting as a copycat of the man I spent interviewing for a year and wrote a book about, I find that unlikely.

Special Agent Harris narrows his eyes and gives me an annoying smirk.

"I guess it's that way with a lot of us." He glances back at the crime scene in front of us. "I read a lot about serial killers when I was a teenager," he says. "I was always the odd kid out at school. But I couldn't get enough of that stuff. I read a ton of John Douglas's work, which I think is pretty standard for anyone at this point who has any interest in this kind of work."

"I've read my fair share of Douglas," I admit. "There's really nobody better than him."

"I actually got to meet him and work with him for a while," Special Agent Harris says. "I'm a profiler myself."

When he says this I look at him. His eyes are trained on the same in front of us.

"So what do you make of this?"

"Well, I don't think it's a bad thing that you're here."

And with that he walks away. Apparently unwilling to share more of his hand than that with me, which I don't blame him for. After all, I am a journalist. And he has every right not to trust me.

"We can get in to see her tomorrow."

I turn and see Parker on my left. He looks at the girl again.

"Well, that's good," I say.

"Yeah," Parker says. "They got her up and around tonight. Talking to her might give us some information that we desperately need." He pauses for a moment, and then looks at me. "I have this gut feeling about this," he says. "Whoever the guy is, he idolizes Nathan Kelly."

I don't say anything right then, but I know what he means about the gut feeling. There's no way this guy isn't inspired by Kelly. Things are just too similar so far. And depending on what that girl tells us tomorrow, they might even get even more similar.

"Are you ready to get some rest?" he asks me.

"You have no idea," I say.

He has another glance back at the girl lying in the ditch, and I do the same thing.

"Let's go."

Parker turns and starts walking for our car, and I follow him, eager to get back in the confines of a safe place like the hotel. And even if it's not safe, at least it feels that way. My mind drifts to whoever might be out at the campground tonight. Specifically any women that might be there.

Parker opens my door, once again acting ever the gentleman. Ghost is happy we're back to the car.

"Your girlfriend must love you," I say, teasingly.

"Ex-wife," he corrects me as he walks around to the other side. We both get in. "She's got strong feelings about me, but I'm not sure I'd call it *love*." He gives me a smirk and turns the car on.

"For some reason, I didn't imagine you'd been married," I say.

"What about you?" He turns the conversation on me.

I see Robert's face. His perfect, chiseled face. And in his Australian accent, I can hear my name. The nickname only he used for me.

Josie.

I furrow my brow and a seething rage bubbles through me. I'd slap his face if I saw him right now. Coward.

I compose myself to answer Parker.

"I had someone," I admit. "On again, off again. That sort of thing. Never really serious, I guess," I remark quietly at the end. It's something about the relationship that I've never really been able to admit to myself. That we must not have been serious.

Who dumps their girlfriend at the Emergency Room

and then leaves? Never to be seen or heard from ever again?

Robert Copperweight. That's who.

The only man I've ever let close enough to truly know me. Even now, as angry as I am at him, he's still the person I would first confide in about anything. And I know it's the same for him. Or at least it was before everything happened.

"I'm sorry," Parker says after a beat of silence. I wonder if he was weighing my words, how I said them. He's an FBI agent, after all.

"I'm sorry you got divorced," I say.

"It's alright," he says softly. But there's a note of pain in his voice.

I don't press it further. We've only just met and I'm not the sort of person that really likes to open up to people. Even ones I've known for quite some time. Robert was the exception to that.

I told him everything.

It's so devastating to realize that someone you once loved can become a perfect stranger and still carry all your secrets inside them. They should have to erase their memory at the end and give those secrets back. I hate the idea of Robert walking around, shooting photos of a war zone, and carrying within him the knowledge of everything that ever hurt me.

It makes me feel far too vulnerable.

At the same time, if something were to happen to

him, he'd take that to his grave. And then there would be no one left with a piece of me.

That thought is equally heartbreaking.

Parker drives us back into town and it passes in a flash, I'm so swept up in memories and complicated feelings. He turns into the parking garage and parks us in the same spot we left earlier.

We get out and head for the hotel, catching an elevator full of people who must have just checked in.

They all smile and step as far aside as they can to let the three of us in. I find myself in front of two young women, both of them wearing puffy jackets and leggings, looking like they're the outdoorsy type.

"...it's just hearsay," one of them whispers to the other.

My ears perk up, almost turning backwards like a dog's, just to hear everything better.

"Still," the other girl says. "I don't know."

"Don't be a little bitch," the first girl whispers. "We can talk about it at the bar later."

And then the elevator dings, and the two of them slither out.

The herd thins as we get closer to our floor, and finally it's just Special Agent Parker and me on the elevator.

It reaches our floor with another satisfying ding and we get off.

"Did you hear those girls?" I ask.

"I kind of tuned them out," Parker admits.

"I think maybe they're planning on going camping," I say as we make our way down the hallway. My room comes up first and Ghost and I stop at the door. Parker turns to face me, stopping, too.

"Really?" He asks.

"Yeah," I say. "I almost felt like I should say something."

"Don't," he says, raising a hand. "The last thing we need is to cause a panic before we have a reason to."

I feel sick at the idea of not warning them.

The one girl sounded so scared. And she has every right to be.

We're almost positive this is a copycat killer.

The campgrounds aren't safe.

"Okay," I say softly, with no intention of listening to Parker.

He nods, seemingly satisfied that he's reined me in. He turns and heads for his room.

"Goodnight," he calls over his shoulder.

And I call back.

"Goodnight."

TEN

I CLOSE the door behind me, and lean back against the surface of it. I slink down, falling into a little pile at the base of it. Ghost licks my face as I take off his harness.

I'm exhausted.

It's well-past midnight at this point. I really need to just take a shower and go to bed.

But the thought of those two girls is like a splinter in the pad of my finger. I'm not going to be able to think about anything else until I get it out. It's a feeling I'm familiar with, and I blame it on having too strong of a conscience. I'm not sure it's actually ethically correct for me to say something to warn anyone at this point, but even though it might not be the ethical thing to do, it feels like the *right* thing to do.

Before I make any decisions, I lean my head back against the door. I bring my wrist up to meet my eyes and note the time: 1:49am.

If those girls have any sense, they'll be getting into bed right now.

If *I* had any sense, I'd be crawling into bed myself. But I sit against the cold metal of the door, feeling it through my sweater. The room is pleasantly cool in the way that only a hotel room can manage to be. Somehow, air conditioned air is colder in a hotel. Maybe it's the industrial strength HVAC units. I'm not sure, but it's not the same anywhere else.

As a kid, I loved staying in hotels. I only got to stay in a couple. Once in grade school when my dad took me with him on a job. Sometimes he had to leave town for one of his handyman jobs. And when I say a *hotel* what I probably mean is a Motel 6 as they were in the mid-nineties.

It was cleaner than home. A trailer in a trailer park on the outskirts of a small city in Oklahoma. My mom usually had beer bottles strewn all across the place. On the floor, on the counters, in the bathroom. If there was a clean surface, she collected her empties there. The trailer smelled like stale beer.

My dad was the bright spot of my childhood, even if he had preferred for me to be a boy.

My mom was always out of reach, her mind covered with the caul of too much to drink. She was somewhere else. Distant and unreachable.

Dad was gruff. A man of few words and not one to really throw around *I love you*'s without careful consideration. In fact, I'm not sure I ever heard him say it.

And then, by the time I was twelve, he was gone.

And it was just me and Mom.

The next hotel I stayed in was in high school. I got to go on a trip with band and we went to Washington, D.C. Somehow, the school got a fully-paid trip to D.C. and we even got to stay at one of the historic hotels. I think another, richer and fancier school sponsored us. But I didn't ask any questions.

I remember lying in the hotel bed, three other girls in the room with me, and feeling safer than I had since my Dad left. Home had become a warzone with Mom.

I think I've always associated hotels with safety and home with danger.

And it's probably one of the reasons I haven't been back since I turned eighteen, even though Mom died last year and the trailer is mine now.

What an inheritance.

These are memories I haven't thought about for a long time. Memories that I usually do a good job tamping down, shoving down, choking back until my eyes water. Because if I don't, I'll cry for the rest of my life.

The best friend I went on vacation with when I was a kid is Jordan. The girl whose mother was murdered by Nathan Kelly.

I'm back in the woods with her, looking at the back of a truck. I grab Jordan's arm to stop her from running forward into certain danger.

Finally, I gasp in the darkened hotel room, and realize where I am right now.

A hand goes to my chest and I feel my own pulse racing.

I inhale, hearing the psych ward therapist count us down in a breathing exercise as I do.

I exhale. 4, 3, 2, 1.

Ghost licks my face furiously and puts his paw on my leg to tell me I need to calm down. He's alerting a panic attack.

I reach up behind me and flip the switch that turns on the entry light in the room, and take in my surroundings. The room has two queen beds in it, a nightstand between them and another light switch on the wall that I assume turns on the lamp on the desk.

Feeling like I weigh a thousand pounds, I grunt as I stand, and both my knees pop. Ghost watches me carefully.

I step into the bathroom and turn on the lights. They're too bright at first and I squint as my eyes adjust. I look like hell, bags sagging under my eyes and my hair looking like it needs a wash. It's been a long time since I was on Good Morning Today, and I'm more than ready for bed.

I start getting my toiletries together to take a shower and as I'm brushing my teeth, I think about the two girls in the elevator.

I stop mid-stroke in brushing my teeth and stare at myself in the mirror. They said they'd be in the bar later. It's closing in on 2:15am and I'm probably going to have to get up at the ass crack of dawn, what difference does it make if I miss another hour of sleep. It won't even be that much, I tell myself.

I spit into the sink and then wash my face quickly, drying it with the hand towel sitting beside the little hotel sink. I take one more look at myself and even though I have a headband holding my hair back, I toss the towel on the sink and head for the door.

The elevator is empty and when Ghost and I reach the lobby, everything is silent aside from two voices coming from the distant side of the lobby. Immediately, I head that direction. The lobby yawns open into a large bar on one side and immediately I spot the two girls, the hesitant one still wearing her puffy coat, stirring a mixed drink in front of herself. Her friend's back is to me and she's speaking animatedly to her friend in the coat. The girl in the coat smiles and laughs at whatever her friend is saying.

I make a beeline for them and the girl in the coat spots me approaching. The look on her face tells me that she's wary of what tidings I'm bringing.

"Hi," I say as I arrive at their table.

The girl that was just talking turns to see me and looks annoyed. She glances at Ghost.

"I'll be quick," I say. "I heard you guys talking in the elevator and I'm not supposed to say anything, but you guys should be careful."

They share a glance.

"Are you trying to scare us?" The girl not wearing her coat asks. Her face cracks into a smile.

"No," I say. "Maybe. Just don't go camping."

I glance at the girl still wearing her coat. She looks terrified. And I'm satisfied with that.

"My name's Josephine," I tell them. I can't say more than that, I imagine. If Parker's name wasn't on the line, I'd tell them exactly what I'm doing here. I consider doing it anyway for a moment. "What are your names?" I ask.

After another shared glance the hesitant one speaks first.

"Amber," she says.

I nod, then look at her friend.

"Jamie," she says, eying me suspiciously. "How do you know something's going on?"

I sigh, irritated with the question. Isn't the warning enough?

"I don't," I lie. "I just have a gut feeling," I say.

"I have a gut feeling, too," Amber says. "I told you that, Jamie." She says sounding disgusted with her friend.

"I'm not forcing you to do anything," Jamie spits back.

"Look, I'm not trying to start a fight between y'all," I say. "I just heard you talking about camping and the girl that came out of the woods. I know what people are saying online about all of this. And I just don't think you should go camping." I shrug. "I just wanted to tell you that."

Amber nods silently, her brow furrowed, and gives me an imploring look, almost like she's begging me to do more to convince Jamie. She looks so young. Both of them do. College-aged. Maybe they both just graduated. Maybe this is a trip they've been planning for a while.

"I'll leave y'all alone," I tell them.

And I turn, headed out of the bar. I catch the bartender's eye as I head out and he gives me a nod, but there's a look on his face making me think he wonders why I came all the way down here not to order a drink. I offer him a pressed smile and continue back to the elevator.

Back at my room, I embrace the quiet. And the fact that I've done all I can do.

I could have told them more.

At Special Agent Parker's peril.

Something like that could affect not only his career, but maybe the investigation itself. Surely I scared both of them enough that they're not going to chance it. Jesus, girls. Go *anywhere* else.

I turn the shower on and slip out of my clothes, reaching my arm into the shower until the water is scalding hot. I want to wash off the day, and any lingering remnants of the smell from the scene. Even though I know it's unlikely that I smell like the corpse, I feel like the scent is stuck in my nostrils.

The same way the scent of espresso used to get stuck in my nose when I worked at Starbucks.

It took a month after I quit for my sense of smell to go back to normal. I worked there for two years, and I was only next to that woman's body for about fifteen minutes. It was *that* potent.

Once the shower is sufficiently hot, I step in. I pour an ample amount of shampoo into my palm and throw it into my hair, massaging all of it into a big lump of hair and suds on the top of my head. I rinse and repeat, something I normally never do. And just as I'm beginning to rinse out the white suds in my hair, a little bit slides down my forehead and right into my left eye.

The burning sensation creeps up on me. It isn't instant. But once it starts to burn, enough soap has gotten in my eye that I know it's not going to stop anytime soon. I force my face under the hot water of the shower head and force my eyes open, blinking them quickly to try and let a little water in.

And just like that, I'm back in that memory. I'm with Jordan, and I'm staring at the back of a pickup truck.

Jordan is struggling with me, trying to get out of my grasp. I squeeze her arm as hard as I can and look back at the truck. I see Gloria's bare foot sticking out of the tailgate.

Jordan starts to call out and I clap a hand over her mouth.

She wants to save her mother, but I can't let her.

He can't know we're here.

My eyes shoot open and scalding water is burning my skin.

I struggle to catch my breath, feeling like I've been

running a marathon. Or through the woods, away from someone like Nathan Kelly.

Just then, I hear a pounding at my door.

ELEVEN

"JOSEPHINE?!" A male voice calls from out in the hallway. I'm immediately struck with fear, thinking of the two voices I was just hearing. Danger. Imminent. Close.

I spin quickly on my heel in the shower and slip, falling down and hitting my chin on the edge of the bathtub. A tooth chips in the process and my tongue finds the jagged edge of it instantly. One of my front teeth, too. Goddammit.

"Josephine!" Another thunderous knock comes at the door. Ghost barks.

It's then that it occurs to me who it is: Lucas Parker.

"I'm in here," I croak, feeling weaker than I have in a long time. I struggle to find my footing and pull the shower level all the way to the left, shutting it off.

My skin radiates the heat that's been pouring onto it for some undefined period of time. I struggle my way out of the bath and grab a towel. And just as I'm doing so, I hear the hotel door open, a couple of voices, and then the bathroom door opens.

I clutch my towel in all the right places to cover myself.

"Joseph—" Agent Parker sees me and immediately covers his eyes and steps back into the hotel room, closing the door behind him with a swiftness. "Sorry!" he calls. "I got worried when you weren't answering your phone or the door."

"How did you get in here?" I ask, trying to sound more amused than horrified.

"I got a key from the front desk," he says. Ghost comes to the door and whines. He paws at it, wanting to get to me.

"Is that something the FBI does regularly?" I call back at him. "Do I need to be worried about you standing over me watching me sleep?"

I hear him sigh through the frosted glass door of the bathroom.

"Won't happen again," he promises. "I thought something had happened to you."

His instincts aren't wrong. Something did happen to me. I glance in the mirror and grin, taking in my new chipped tooth smile. Not terrible. It could be fixed if I had the time.

Maybe it's my history with men who think they know what's best for me, but the thought that Parker would just swing by the front desk and get a key to my room with whatever FBI black magic he had to use is not only irritating but also chilling.

The thought brings Robert to mind.

And the hospital.

And the way he just ghosted me after he dropped me off.

My mom used to say that Dad running off was what was best for me in the long run. And that he knew that, too. She insisted that was why he left. But I always figured it was her who ran him off. I spent most of my teen years romanticizing the man that had left us to fend for ourselves. Not that my mother was any angel.

I wrap the towel around myself and take in the appearance of my skin.

Hot pink, red in some places. It stings and feels raw to the touch. As I dry off, each movement feels like my skin is stretching to its limits across my muscles. I feel like liquid inside a stainless steel cup left out in the sun for a day.

I overdid it.

I open the door and peer out into my hotel room.

Parker's gone. Or so it seems. I can't fight the feeling that I'm being watched now. He's made certain of that. Maybe that was his end up. Maybe he wasn't worried about me at all. But when I walk over to the nightstand and check my phone, I realize it's already 9am.

Jesus. How long was I in there.

I do the same thing at home sometimes. Dissociate in a scalding hot shower.

But the difference at home is that the water runs cold. That didn't happen in the hotel. I imagine they keep a ton of water heated at any given time.

I see a note scrawled on the notepad next to my phone and pick it up.

Meet me downstairs when you're ready. Sincerely sorry about that.

The written apology does little to quell my irritation. I could use another one in person. Spoken. Straight to my face. But if I'm being honest with myself, it won't make a difference.

If I learned one thing from my mother, it was how to hold, nurture, and carry a grudge from one century to the next. I tell myself I need to let it go. I'm not even going to be here that long in all likelihood. It doesn't matter, I assure myself.

I glance over my shoulder and around the room, just to be sure that I'm alone, even though I know with certainty Lucas Parker isn't hiding in here. Ghost is at my side, making sure I'm okay.

Maybe it's the combination of staying too long in the shower with the shock of someone coming into my room that's putting me on high alert. Hyperaware of my surroundings, I tell myself to calm down. It's a trauma response, a therapist told me. Hyper-vigilance, I think he called it. I didn't see him long. Only during the time I was in the psych ward after Robert dumped me there.

I wonder what he tells all the girls that have come after me.

She was crazy.

Intense.

Nuts.

A real pain in my ass.

"At least I got one good thing out of it," I tell Ghost. He looks up at me and tilts his head, aware I'm giving him a compliment, it seems. Like he's saying, *Who? Me?*

I get ready quickly, conscious of the fact that I'm making Parker wait. That dissociation shouldn't have happened. It's been a long time since I've had one in the shower like that. After I throw on a flannel shirt and some jeans, I check my complexion in the mirror. I'm still pink and raw like I've spent all day floating down the lazy river with no sunscreen.

I remember wondering, as a kid, what a lazy river was. Some of the girls at school would go to White Water Bay each summer. My family couldn't afford it, and I was never invited anyway. It wasn't until I was an adult that I experienced a theme park attraction like that. Even as an adult, it felt magical. Despite knowing that all the little kids there had probably peed in the water, or worse, I found myself enchanted with the whole idea of a theme park. Disney is still on my bucket list.

There's something about a place like that. It invites you to suspend disbelief in a way that's not possible in the real world. It's one of the closest things to magic you can get in the real world.

"Come on," I tell Ghost as I grab his harness and leash. He stands still, content to let me slip on the harness and attach the leash. The harness is glow in the dark, a pale neon green during daylight hours and bright at night. I make out the black lettering on one of his patches: GIVE US SPACE with a UFO embroidered above.

Far too many people are comfortable with crowding service dogs. I could do without that.

After Ghost is ready to go, we step out into the hallway and make our way to the elevator and then downstairs. I spot Parker at a breakfast table across from the bar. He sees me coming and raises a hand to wave. As we approach, he stands until I get seated.

He's already got his own breakfast out in front of him.

"They got anything good?" I ask, giving Ghost a pat on the head as he settles down under my feet.

"Scrambled eggs and pancakes. Not bad. Pretty good for a hotel breakfast, if you ask me," Parker says, then takes a sip of coffee.

"Stay," I tell Ghost, and get up from my chair. I head over to the breakfast bar and get some food. Eggs, pancakes, fruit. I grab an orange juice, even though I should probably have as much caffeine as possible.

I return to the table and dig in.

"What's on the schedule for today?" I ask Parker between bites.

He swallows and takes a sip of coffee.

"Well," he says. "I actually thought I might have you walk me through your research. I've read your book, but I want you to walk me through it. I need to know everything you know, even the stuff you left out. I'm certain this guy is a copy cat and Nathan Kelly is his hero."

"Hard to imagine that guy being someone's hero," I mutter, even though I know it's a thing that happens. Generally, though, the people who idolize serial killers are teens testing the boundaries of the psyche, trying to figure out who they are, and they usually grow out of it. But there's the odd one that doesn't. I don't think there's anything wrong with being fascinated by these people, but there is something very wrong with glorifying them to the point that the shoes they were executed in are worth $5,000.

Murderabilia is a thing within the true crime community. Some people are disgusted by it, others find it too tempting. Some sellers have pieces like bricks from Jeffrey Dahmer's apartment building after it was torn down. Others have original Pogo paintings by John Wayne Gacy. There's even a museum in Las Vegas with some serial killer's toenail clippings.

Wanting those things is beyond me.

But maybe that's because I come to my connection to serial killers honestly.

I was right there when the Heartland Hunter got Jordan's mom.

Maybe that's why, as perplexing as I find these individuals, I don't have any desire to own anything that belonged to them or once hung on their body. To each their own, though.

"I think this killer we've got on our hands thinks Kelly

is the bee's knees," Parker says. "Everything so far is by the book when it comes to the way Nathan Kelly tortured and killed his victims. That being said, I want you to take me through your research today. But before that, we have something more pressing. We're going to go speak with the woman that ran out of the woods. She's being released from the hospital today, so we're headed there after breakfast."

I nod, eager to get a chance to talk to her.

No news has been broken about her other than she was naked and found beside the road. Even with that small amount of information available to the public, I figure our guy has to be at least a little nervous.

That's good.

That means he might be in the right headspace to make a mistake.

And that's very good for us, indeed.

TWELVE

PARKER DRIVES and the hospital is close by. Only about a mile from the hotel, actually. Once inside, he tells a girl at a large desk near the entrance who we are and who we're here to see. She nods solemnly and gets on the phone, presumably to let the staff know we'll be coming. She nods at Parker and gestures for the two of us to head for the elevators.

I follow him and once we're on the fourth floor, we're met with a pleasant dinging sound and the doors slide open. There's a nurses' desk just in front of the elevators and Parker introduces us.

"Special Agent Lucas Parker and this is my partner Josephine Larson," he says, surprising me with his use of terminology. I'm not sure the FBI would be so keen on him throwing the word *partner* around, but for some reason, I like it.

"Partner, huh?" I tease him as the nurse shows us to the woman's room.

Parker brushes me off.

"Her name is Elizabeth Wheatley," he says. "She's a college student. She was camping, hoping to make her way down the west coast, all the way to Los Angeles. But her trip was cut short."

I nod, just as solemn as the girl that told us to take the elevator up to see Elizabeth. I wonder what exactly we're walking into. The room is in ICU. And the nurse raps three times on the door, then slowly pushes it open. The room inside is dark, but I hear voices coming from the television.

"Knock, knock, Elizabeth," the nurse says as she pushes the door in. "I've got some people that would like to speak to you."

Elizabeth says nothing, but the nurse leads us in anyway.

When we come around the corner of the bathroom, I see her.

She's skin and bone, her hair falling out in places. It looks like it's been washed recently, though. Probably after she got to the hospital. Her body is covered in scars and bruises, many of them looking quite recent. I notice a mark on her arm that reminds me of the crime scene photos involving some of Kelly's victims. The very same kind of mark they would have after he used them as a practice target for darts.

One of her eyes is healing from a punch, the bruising yellow and green with only a hint of purple now.

I offer her a kind smile as we step up to the foot of her bed.

She draws her eyes from the television and stares at me. There's something missing. Even though the girl isn't more than twenty-two, she looks hollowed. Like she's lived ten lifetimes and seen all the worst the earth has to offer.

And I have no doubt she has.

Especially if this guy is a Kelly copycat.

"Hi, Elizabeth," I say. Parker stands quietly at my side. "I'm Josephine Larson."

She just eyes me suspiciously.

"I already talked to the cops," she says.

"I'm not a cop," I tell her.

"He looks like a cop," she says, nodding at Parker.

"He's not really a cop, either," I assure her. She still looks less than certain that she wants to talk to us. "And I understand you've been through more in the last few days than anyone should ever go through in a lifetime. We just wanted to talk to you."

"I guess you can," Elizabeth says, softening a little. "Who are you?"

"I'm a researcher and a journalist," I tell her. "I wrote a book about a guy that did things like what was done to you."

At that statement, I see fear shine in her eyes at the mere recollection of what was done to her. I instantly feel regret for putting it so boldly. I should have kneecapped that somehow, softened it a bit. But it's too late.

"The FBI brought me in because there are a lot of similarities," I tell her.

I glance at Parker and he gives me a look that lets me know I've said more than I should.

"We just have a few questions for you," he says. "We'll be as quick as we can be."

She nods, seeming to be content with this arrangement.

Parker looks at me.

"Can you remember anything that happened before you were found on the side of the highway?" I ask Elizabeth.

"Yeah," she says. "I remember everything."

"What happened to you?"

"I'd been camping in a tent at the RV park. I was making a trip down the west coast," she says. "Just a stupid thing I wanted to do after graduating," she says, her voice full of regret. "It was the second night camping there that it happened. I went to the bathroom and left my tent. I noticed this guy across the way, dressed all in black, he kind of looked at me and waved. But there was something about him that gave me a bad vibe. I hurried to the bathroom. After I was done, I looked around for him before walking back to my tent. I even debated on moving that night. Just packing up and continuing to drive. But I didn't see him and I decided to stay. I thought maybe he was just passing by. I went to bed, not thinking anything of it. Then at about 2:00 in the morning, the zipper of my tent goes down. I hear the sound of it. I was freaking out. Terrified. I knew a bear wouldn't use the zipper. I fumbled around for something. I had a pocket knife but that was it. He grabbed me by the feet and before I could scream, he hit me over the head, hard."

"Did he knock you out?" I ask.

"Yeah," Elizabeth says. "The next thing I remember is waking up in the dark. I was in the back of a truck, it seemed like. And there was a gag in my mouth. My hands and feet were tied and he'd put a blanket over me. I tried to scream, but all that came out was a muffled attempt at a scream."

Elizabeth pauses, her brows furrowing as she remembers. My heart beats a little faster in my chest, imagining her experience and remembering Jordan's mom. I remind myself that this isn't the same guy. This is a copycat. Someone who wants to emulate Nathan Kelly. I'm safe.

"Where did he take you?" I ask.

"It seemed like he drove forever," she says. Her brow relaxes for a moment. "The road got rougher, like maybe he wasn't on the main highway anymore. My best guess would be that we kept going for over three hours, but honestly, I don't know that my sense of time during all of that can be trusted," she says. "Finally, we stopped. He got out of the vehicle and then opened the tailgate. I could barely move. He picked me up and carried me into a shed," she says as the furrow returns to her brow. She hesitates.

"Was that where he kept you?" I ask.

"Yes," she says softly. "It was a small shed. No windows, concrete walls. I don't think anyone would have heard me scream out there. I tried at first. He just laughed. 'Girl, no one out here is gonna hear you. You're a hundred miles from anything.' That's what he said."

I glance at Parker, making note of the comment that she was a hundred miles from anything. If they drove for three hours, he might have been able to cover more than 150 miles, so his statement would be about right.

"What happened after he put you there?" I ask.

"He starved me, tortured me, raped me," she says, her tone lifeless as she recounts the events from that basement with a hollow, clinical tone.

"I know this is difficult to talk about," I say. "But how did he torture you?"

She winces at the question. I feel horrible for asking, but we need to know. I glance at Parker and he gives me a nod of reassurance, telling me I'm doing the right thing. It doesn't feel that way. I turn my focus back to Elizabeth.

"He used me for entertainment," she says quietly. Her voice shakes. "As a dart board. A human punching bag. He would practice his dart-throwing skills on me." She glances at the mark on her arm that I thought might have been from just that activity. "One of his favorite things to do would be to make me piss myself. He would keep me from using the bathroom for long periods of time. And then he would taunt me because I was begging to go to the bathroom, handing me a bucket. Other times, he would beat it out of me. That's when he wasn't raping me," she says.

The detail about the torture disturbs me. It's something that was specific to Nathan Kelly. I remember Kelly talking about it. The look in his eyes when he did. That was more disturbing than hearing the acts themselves.

"I am so sorry this happened to you. You didn't deserve it," I tell Elizabeth.

She looks at me, and I can't tell if she wants to thank me for the comment or tell me to fuck off.

"He's gonna do it to someone else, you know?"

Her words hang between me and Parker. We both know this. It's the whole reason we're here. I don't want to put it that way to Elizabeth, though.

"You sharing your experience with us might help bring this to an end more quickly," Parker says delicately. "You're being very brave."

Elizabeth looks between the two of us.

"What else do you want to know?" she asks.

"Do you remember anything distinctive about the journey out there or anything about the place once you got there?" Parker asks.

Elizabeth hesitates for a moment.

"There was still a Christmas tree up in his living room. It was in front of the window," she says.

"Was it lit?" Parker asks.

"Yeah," Elizabeth says. "He never bothered to unplug it."

The detail reminds me of a time when my mom was

in rehab, back before Dad left. He didn't bother to put the tree away while she was gone, even though he knew she wanted him to. I think he did it to spite her. They really hated each other sometimes.

"Was there anyone else there?" I ask.

"No. Just me and him," Elizabeth says. "It felt like forever. But according to the math, it was two months from the day I went missing to when I stumbled out onto the highway."

"How did you escape?" I ask.

"I didn't, really. After he'd had his fun with me, he told me it was time to put me out to pasture."

It's a phrase that Nathan Kelly used. I feel a chill ascend my spine.

"He took me into the woods, naked, and told me to run as far and fast as I could. That he was giving me a head start. I had fifteen minutes, and then he'd come after me, rifle in hand."

"He hunted you?" Parker asks.

"Yeah," Elizabeth says. "He hunted me."

"What happened then?" I ask.

"I picked a direction and I ran," she says. "I was so weak, but I used every bit of strength I had. I thought about my mom and my little sister. I couldn't leave them behind. I couldn't let him kill me. I just kept running. I ran until I couldn't feel my legs. My entire body was cold to the point of numbness. I fell, but I got up and kept running. It was like something else took over. And then I heard traffic," she says. "I stopped to listen, just to make sure. I could hear a highway. It was dark then. I don't know how many hours passed or how far I ran. But apparently we weren't a hundred miles from everything. Or at least we weren't that far from the highway. I heard him then in the distance. He whistled. The same whistling he would do as he made his way down to the basement, one step at a time. It was the same. So calm, casual. He thought he had me. I ran harder and faster through the woods. I tripped and stumbled several times. My feet were bleeding at this point. The sound of the highway was getting closer and closer. And then I could see the headlights through the trees in front of me. I stumbled out onto it, naked and afraid, and I threw myself to my knees, waving my hands over my head as a semi-truck barreled towards me. He stopped with me in his headlights. And that's how I got here," she says.

The whistling.

It was something distinctive about Nathan Kelly. He'd taunt his victims in the same way, conditioning them to the sound so that they associated it with the terror he put them through. And then, as he stalked them through the woods, he would make the same noise. More than anything, Kelly loved tormenting women. He loved the sense of power that came with that for him.

I think this guy gets the same buzz out of it.

"Did he ever mention anything to you about Nathan Kelly?" Parker asks.

"Who's that?" the girl asks.

I glance at Parker.

"I think that's all the questions we've got for you," he says to her.

"Thank you for answering them," I add. "Take care of yourself, Elizabeth."

She nods at me, but that same hollow look that she had in her eyes when we first arrived is back. She's checking out again. I can hardly blame her.

Parker shakes her hand and I do the same. Then we head for the door, Ghost right beside me.

THIRTEEN

BACK AT THE POLICE STATION, Parker opens the door for us. Ghost and I pass through and we make our way back to the conference room. Once there, Wilson is eager to talk to Parker.

"Find anything out that we didn't already know?"

Parker glances at me and nods.

I speak.

"The guy whistles, just like Kelly," I tell him.

He looks at me and then at Parker, unsure what I'm referencing.

"Nathan Kelly would whistle at his victims. He would do it when he was ready to use them for whatever purpose he saw fit. He wanted them to associate the sound with terror. This guy is doing the same thing. It's a very specific detail to be copied. This guy really admires Nathan Kelly, I would say," I tell him.

"What do you think, Parker?" Wilson asks, almost dismissing me.

"I think you should listen to her," Special Agent Parker says, taking up for me.

"I can hold my own," I tell Parker politely, then turn my attention to Wilson. "I believe I was asked to be here as an expert," I tell him. "That's my expert opinion, as the person that spent more time with Kelly than anyone else."

Wilson looks at me like he's sizing me up.

"I did bring her here because of that," Parker speaks up.

"Fine," Wilson says. "Did she give you any information that might help us find this guy?"

"We think he must be within 150 miles from here," Parker says. I nod.

"Damn," Wilson says and punches a fist on the table in front of him. "That's not anything we didn't know from the police report."

I glance at Parker, giving him a look that tries to convey that I'm sorry. I feel like I'm getting him in trouble here. He looks back at Wilson.

"We'll stay after him," Parker says.

"You'd better," Wilson says, and stalks off, presumably to get another cup of coffee. It seems that there isn't a lot of sleep going around in these parts.

"I'm sorry about that," I tell Parker.

"Don't be," he says. "He's always like that. You didn't do anything wrong."

"I feel like me coming here hasn't been helpful at all," I tell him.

"No, no," he says, quickly correcting me. He places a hand on my shoulder and I glance over at him. "We're going to figure this out. We just have to wait now," Parker says.

"Wait until someone else turns up dead?" I ask.

Parker doesn't speak immediately.

"What did they find out on the autopsy of the girl beside the highway?" I ask, unwilling to sit idly by.

"Same marks on her body as Elizabeth," Parker says. "I got a call about it this morning. It looks like she was also raped and used for dart target practice, among other things. She was covered in urine and feces, according to the testing."

It sounds so much like the women Kelly killed. One of them was found on the side of the road, dumped only the night before. Much like the girl we saw on the side of the road the other night. The theory at the time was that Kelly didn't find any use for a girl that didn't survive until the final phase of his process. If she died before she could run through the woods, he wanted her out of there as quickly as possible, presumably so he could move on to his next potential victim.

This guy did the same thing.

"There's one thing that I didn't put in the book," I say, surprising myself and Parker.

He arches an eyebrow and his eyes widen. He waits for me to speak.

"It was something that Kelly said to me in passing one day. I didn't think anything of it until now," I say. "He said his favorite color of zip ties was neon yellow. He liked that he could see from across the room whether they were still intact. The color thing never came up with the cops. They didn't have any reason to ask him why that particular color."

Parker rolls this over in his mind.

"The girl the other night. She had one on her wrist. The zip tie was neon yellow," I tell him.

"It was, wasn't it?" Parker asks.

"This guy isn't just a fan of Kelly," I say. "He *knows* him."

PARKER LOOKS at me like it's the first time he's had this thought. I would be lying if I said that I'd had it before. The idea that this copycat could have been in contact with Nathan Kelly didn't occur to me until just now. But the fact that this person used neon yellow zip ties has me talking to myself.

I think about him calling me when I was on my way to Fairbanks. The thought of him in that jail, knowing something that I didn't in that moment. I didn't even think about that as a possibility at the time.

"You think this guy's been communicating with him?" Parker asks.

"He had to be," I say. "There's no way he could've known that otherwise about the zip ties."

"We need to talk to Kelly," Parker says with finality. "Really it's you that needs to talk to Kelly," he adds, looking over at me.

"I knew you were going to say that," I say to Parker with a sad smile. "I really don't relish the idea of talking to the guy."

"You'd never know it with all the time you spent with him," Parker says with a wink.

Part of me wants to admit that every moment with Nathan Kelly was excruciating. Another part of me doesn't want Parker to think I'm soft. He brought me here for a reason. I intend to fulfill my end of the bargain. I just nod and give him a little laugh that tells him I think he's funny.

We spend the next thirty minutes arranging for a phone call with Kelly back in Colorado. For a guy that's locked up he sure is hard to track down for a little video call. It's not lost on anyone that Kelly has probably realized at this point what we've just become aware of. He knows the cops are onto him. And there's no way he doesn't have a connection to this guy. Possibly as a mentor, grooming him into a full-fledged serial killer. And how could Kelly pass it up? This guy seems to worship him. I can't think of any narcissists that would turn that down.

But finally, well into the afternoon, we get a video call from the prison.

Wilson has me sit down in front of the laptop, putting my back to the wall. The idea is to put Kelly as at ease as possible, though he doesn't deserve it. However, without that, we may not get any of the information out of him that we need.

On the screen, it tells me that the other party is joining the call. My stomach drops, all my memories of working with him coming back at once. The way he could make my skin crawl, and how I came back for it every day for a year anyway.

What the hell is wrong with me?

I'm not sure anyone has time for a list that long.

I feel Ghost lay his head on my thigh, the task he's supposed to perform when he senses my anxiety rising. I reach down and stroke his head, his soft white fur warm and silky. I glance down at him and see his pink nose sticking out from under the table and it makes me smile momentarily. And then the video conferencing software makes a dinging noise that startles me out of my comfort zone with Ghost.

"Well, well, well. If it isn't Josephine Larson," Kelly says instead of *hello*. This is the way he operates. He likes to make people uncomfortable from the very beginning of their interactions with him. There's no denying that he's charming, but there's something just beneath the surface that I think would make anyone think twice about going anywhere alone with him.

"Hello, Nathan," I say.

"Nate, please," he tells me in the manner you'd tell

someone to call you by your informal nickname for the thousandth time. Like we're old friends and he can't believe I'd use anything other than the diminutive.

"How are you doing?" I ask him, eager to shift the focus onto him. The last thing I want is for this to devolve into something I don't have control over. Kelly's notorious for that. He managed it more than a few times when I was researching my book.

"Can't complain," he says. "Let me guess. You're in Alaska."

He flips it right back around on me without warning and it puts me off guard.

"What makes you think that?" I ask, feeling a little creeped out at how perceptive Kelly is sometimes.

He looks into the camera and scoots closer, almost like he's leaning against a table to make his point.

"Oh, you didn't think you could get anything past me, did you?" He's only half-teasing when he says it. I swallow, my mouth feeling dry. It's shocking to me how much of an effect he has on me even now. There was a period of time where I got too comfortable in his presence. It didn't take him long to remind me who was calling the shots. After that, I kept a wall up between us.

"You? Never," I say, stroking Ghost's head and telling myself to cool down.

"So, how's Fairbanks?" Kelly asks.

"Nice. Cool," I say. "Better than Oklahoma this time of year."

"You working with the police up there? Tryin' to catch you a copycat?"

"What makes you think I'm working with the police?" I ask.

"It's been all over the news," he says with a snort. "I'm not a mind-reader, Josephine. I saw it on the television. You and some good-lookin' suit went to dinner the other night. It's all anybody's talkin' about in here. My biographer and the copycat. Spooky stuff, if you ask me."

Kelly gives a little performative shiver and smirks at me.

I glance at Parker standing across the table in front of me. He gives me a nod, letting me know I'm not alone. *Keep going. I'm here.* I look back at Kelly.

"Oh, is he with you right *now*?" Kelly asks. He whistles and it sends a chill through me. The whistle he used to terrorize women with. "He must be a special one, the way you go through 'em."

I bristle at the comment.

"I'm not sure what you mean," I say, but my voice falters. I realize that I need to turn the conversation back around, and I'm about to when he speaks.

"How's Robert?" Kelly asks.

My heart races and I feel a flush of blood hit my cheeks. They're warm, heating up as he stares at me. It's an intimate question. Inappropriate, regardless of how he knows that Robert was once a part of my life. As far as he knows, we did that story together.

"Oh, haven't you talked to him recently?" Kelly asks, reading my silence and the flush on my face.

"We don't talk much anymore," I say, trying to remain composed, but the words come out through gritted teeth. I swallow, conscious of the movement in my throat, wondering if he notices it. Who am I kidding? Kelly notices everything. It's his superpower. It's almost otherworldly. If he wasn't a serial killer, he might be able to make a living as a psychic doing cold reads.

"That's a shame. That article y'all did together was good. I re-read it sometimes. Especially when I miss you," he says, adding the last with a wink that makes my skin crawl.

"Listen, Nathan," I say. "I need to know what you know about what's happening up here."

He shakes his head and furrows his brows.

"Well, I don't know much other than what I've seen in the news. A copycat. I'm flattered," he adds with a smile.

"Cut the bullshit," I say, growing irritated with his performance.

"I'm not sure what you mean," Kelly says. He leans closer to the camera. "I don't know *shit* about whatever the fuck is going on up there. But I do know one thing," he says. "It ain't stoppin' anytime soon. Not 'til you catch the guy, Joey."

The nickname makes me want to disappear inside myself. The only person who ever called me that was my father. I usually correct people right away when they make the mistake of using it. But there's something about the way Kelly says it that makes me feel like it's intentional. Like he's using a nickname to pull some sort of reaction out of me. I steel my nerves.

"It would be in your best interest to tell someone if you know anything," I say evenly.

"Why?" Kelly asks with a laugh. "Am I gonna get released on good behavior, you think?"

There's venom in his tone. He knows he's never getting out of prison unless he's in a body bag. We both know that.

His cooperation wouldn't benefit him at all.

"Even if I did know somethin'," he says. "I wouldn't tell you. You're a smart one, Joey. You always could read me. And I felt like we had somethin' special when we worked together on that book."

"*I* wrote that book. *We* didn't."

"It wouldn't exist if I hadn't raped and killed all them pretty girls," he says. "In a way, I made you famous, Joey."

My breathing grows shallower and more rapid. Rage is bubbling just beneath the surface.

I reach up and slam the laptop shut without bothering to say goodbye.

I push my seat back from the table and cover my face with my hands.

"*Fuck*," I mutter.

Parker comes around to me, placing a hand on my back. Ghost paws at my leg and stands on it, nuzzling at my face and licking me. I look up and acknowledge him, telling him he's a good boy.

"You want some water?" Parker asks.

"Yes, please," I say.

Wilson sighs, evidently irritated that we didn't make more progress than that with Kelly.

"I'll send some agents to talk to him," he says to me with as much concern as he can muster. I just nod. I don't feel like there's anything I can say to make it better. Wilson turns and walks off, fetching his cell phone out of his pocket, presumably to call the main office and bitch about the journalist Parker insisted on bringing in.

Parker comes back with a bottle of water. I press the cold plastic to my face and then unscrew the cap, taking a long drink.

"I'm sorry about that," I say.

"Don't apologize," Parker says. "I didn't have any high hopes that Kelly would cooperate. Maybe having a couple of FBI agents show up might make him a little more eager to spill," he suggests with a shrug.

I doubt it, though. Kelly has an iron will. He's not someone that I think police pressure works on. He knows he's in prison for the rest of his life and then some. He was sentenced to thirteen life sentences. I imagine, if he does have anything to do with the copycat, he doesn't feel like he has a lot to lose by keeping the guy's secrets.

"I'm sure he knows who it is," I say. "Or has some idea. I wonder if he's been corresponding with anyone lately."

"I'll find out," Parker says. He pulls out his phone and makes a note.

"I wish I was more help," I tell him.

"Don't worry about it," he says. "I still have some work for you to do," he adds with a smile.

"I'm not sure if I should be excited or terrified," I joke.

"It won't be too bad. Why don't we get out of here? We'll go somewhere we can talk," he says. He glances around. The energy in the conference room isn't as ebullient as it was when I first arrived. In a couple of days, the cops and the feds have run into a few dead ends. There was some forensic evidence found on the girl beside the road, but they won't have the info back on that from the lab for a while.

Hopefully sooner rather than later.

FOURTEEN

BACK AT THE hotel I grab my laptop before we head out. Parker picks a bar across the street that has a quiet atmosphere. The doors look like they were ripped right out of an old saloon. They swing on their hinges as we enter. The place is dark. A jukebox sits in the corner and a couple of men are playing pool across from the bar. Ghost tucks himself neatly under the table.

Parker grabs us each a beer and we head for a booth where I crack open my laptop, accessing all of my research notes from the time when I was interviewing Nathan Kelly on a daily to weekly basis.

He takes a sip of his beer and I do the same.

"Where would you like for me to start?" I ask.

"Start at the beginning. You've got a personal connection to Kelly, right?" Parker says.

"My best friend's mom was his first known victim," I confirm.

Parker nods, having already read this in the book. I guess he just wanted to hear it from me.

"You went camping that night with your friend and her mom," Parker continues for me. "Her mom went to the bathroom at the campsite and she never came back. I can't imagine what that must have been like for your friend, or you for that matter."

"Horrible," I say. "To make a long story short. Jordan was never okay again."

I find myself going quiet after the mention of Jordan. I haven't talked to her in years. I wanted to interview her for the book, but she turned me down.

"I understand why you want to write it, but I just can't," she'd said.

"People tell you to *get over it* when someone dies after awhile," I say. "After it's no longer fresh, they expect you to get back to who you were before the loss. I think what happened to her mother was next level. It wasn't just death. It was murder in its coldest sense. For the pleasure of someone else. How do you get past that if you're the one that's left behind?" I ask, making eye contact with Parker.

"You don't," Parker says simply. "Of all the people I've worked with, I don't think any of them are the person they were before something like that happened. I don't think you ever get over it."

"I don't either. And Jordan definitely didn't. She dropped out of school in tenth grade. She was skipping school and hanging out with some of the kids that were known to do harder drugs than just weed. She got it together in the last few years, but mostly because she had a kid," I say. "But there's no light in her eyes anymore," I add, and then grow quiet.

"When something like that happens, it's the starkest reminder that the things that keep us safe in society are rules and laws that we've collectively agreed upon, for the most part. For most of us, that's enough to keep us in line. A sense of right and wrong and societal pressure. But for some people, that's not enough. For some people, it's just a suggestion."

I think about Kelly. He was a habitual law-breaker in every way he could be. He wasn't like other serial killers that played things by the book to the point that everyone in their lives was shocked to learn who they really were. It wasn't like that for Kelly.

The people that knew him told me they'd always had a feeling. Or that Kelly just had an energy that put them off to such a degree that they made a point not to be alone with him.

If there had been a Most Likely to Murder title in his senior yearbook, he'd have won it hands down according to the people that knew him.

Laws *were* just a suggestion for Kelly.

Including all the ones about murder.

I take a deep breath.

"That just affected me so much as a kid. I could never let it go. I always felt like maybe there was some way that I could have saved Jordan," I say.

"You couldn't have," Parker assures me, leaning across the table. "Telling the story is the best thing you can do," he says.

"The best thing I can do is stop what's happening now," I correct him.

Parker takes a deep breath.

"You feel the same," I say. "You want to figure this out as much as I do. The idea that someone mimicking Kelly could be out there is enough to make me never want to sleep again," I say.

"You and me both," Parker says, but he sounds resigned. "We need a fresh lead," he admits.

"Hard to wish for something like that when it usually means someone else has to go missing," I remark.

Parker nods, acknowledging the truth of this.

"Maybe something else will come up, though," I say, trying to instill some hope back into the conversation.

"Maybe so," Parker says. "Until then," he says with a clap of his hands. "Let's go over your notes. See if there's anything in there that could possibly point us in a new direction."

"I'm game," I say.

My body is exhausted. I need sleep. But this is important. I'm not sure that I've ever had an opportunity like this before in my life. The opportunity to right old wrongs. To do justice for Jordan and her mother, and stop this creep who thinks he's some kind of god, deciding which women live and die in the campgrounds he stalks.

"Where do you want me to start?" I ask. "Now that we've covered the very beginning."

Parker sighs, his eyes tired. I wonder if he's as exhausted as I am.

"Start with the first time you met him," he says.

The memory sends a chill over me. I'm not sure I could have completed the book if it wasn't because of my personal connection to things. That was driving me the whole time. Otherwise, I wouldn't have spent another second in Kelly's presence.

"Alright," I say. "But to get there, I probably need to tell another story first."

Then I take a deep breath, glance at my notes, and begin to tell Parker the story.

FIFTEEN

ROBERT IS relevant to the tale, so I start there.

After I'd all but given up on seeing him again, I saw him in South Dakota.

I was working on a story about the pipeline and the place was crawling with journalists. The hotels and motels in the area were packed to the rafters with our kind. Protestors were everywhere. The story needed to be told from ground zero, and I was up for the challenge.

I'd been interviewing people and going out every day to talk to the protestors and the organizers. I'd gotten a bunch of them to sit down with me and go on the record. I'd taken pictures and the story was developing. And that's when I ran into Robert.

I spotted him one day at the protests.

He was shooting photos of the crowd. Getting individual portraits of some of the people there. I was midway through asking questions in an interview with one of the organizers, following up on some things we'd talked about the day before. And just like that, he was standing not five yards away.

"So, is that what—" I stopped mid-sentence, staring at a man I thought I'd never see again.

"Everything okay?" The organizer followed my gaze. "What's up?" She asked me, turning back to face me. I was still staring at Robert.

"I know him," I told her, turning to face her. "I know him and I need to go," I said. I had no idea what else to say. My brain had short-circuited. So many things were happening in my head all at once.

I left my things sitting at the makeshift interview station I'd prepared, and I walked toward Robert. He was looking through the lens of his camera, shooting shot after shot to the point that I could hear the shutter fluttering when I walked up beside him.

"Hey," I said.

Robert brought his camera down and looked at me.

"Holy *shit*," he said, letting his camera drop to his side. He wrapped me in a huge hug and picked me up off my feet, spinning me around. "What the hell are you doing here?"

"The same thing you are," I told him with a wide grin.

"How the hell have you been?" Robert asked, his eyes hungry for the sight of me. He looked me up and down. "You look fantastic."

"I've been good," I told him. At the time, it was the

truth. Things had been good. I'd missed him, though. And there was the faintest bit of sting in the way he left things. He'd just sort of disappeared. "How are you?" I asked, redirecting the focus of the conversation.

"I've been phenomenal," he said. "Just traveling, covering stories."

"I can't believe you're actually right here," I said, staring at him, the smile fading from my face and being replaced with a more serious expression. His smile faded then, too. And just like that, he kissed me, grabbing the sides of my face and pressing his lips to mine like his life depended on it. Like I was oxygen and he'd just surfaced after almost drowning.

He pulled away and looked down at me.

"Let's get out of here," he said.

I was shocked slightly by the suggestion. We shouldn't have left. But we did. As much as I wanted to be a good journalist, I wanted Robert more.

We went to a roadside bar only a few miles from the protest. I'd packed up my laptop and my camera and backpack and piled them into Robert's rental car, then he drove us to the first bar that we found.

It was a biker place. An aluminum barn-like building that had been converted into a dark bar with plenty of neon signs for various types of beer on the wall. They had music, cold beer, and the neon provided somewhat romantic lighting.

We talked all afternoon and into the evening. I drank, and drank, and drank. And we laughed so much.

Finally, I felt comfortable enough to broach the subject of his disappearance. Our laughter was fading from the last thing that Robert said and there was a lull in the conversation. I couldn't help myself.

"Why did you disappear?" I asked him, taking a sip of my beer and holding the bottle by the neck. I looked into his eyes. He sighed, a sad smile curving his lips.

"You're a good person, Jo," he said. "Africa with you is one of the memories I'll be playing back in my mind when I'm an old man on my deathbed."

The image made me chuckle, but there was also something sad about it.

"But you deserve better than me," he said. He took a drink of his beer.

"Why would you say that?" I asked.

"I'm not the kind of guy that you marry," he said. "I'm never going to settle down. I'm never going to get married, have kids, a house. None of that."

"What makes you think I want any of that?" I asked, feeling indignant. "Are you assuming just because I'm a woman, I'm looking for a man to tie down with all those things? Do you think *I* want to be tied down like that?"

Robert laughed at my animation.

"You deserve to be with someone who wants that with you," he said.

"You're not listening to me."

"*You're* not listening to *me*," he said with a smirk.

"What are you trying to say?" I asked.

"That I'm not the one," Robert said with a laugh.

"But you? You'd be the one to any guy with an ounce of sense."

"But not to you?" I asked, feeling a surge of emotion I wasn't expecting.

He stood up and pulled his seat up next to mine. Our arms touched and he whispered in my ear.

"I'm afraid I wouldn't be enough," he said softly.

I turned to face him. He brought his hand up to my face and traced his thumb across my lower lip. God, he was beautiful. I stared into his eyes and lost myself there. Then he leaned down and kissed me softly.

We made out in the bar. I didn't care who was around. All that mattered was that, after all this time, I'd found Robert again. He was here, now, with me. It didn't matter what he was saying. He didn't *know* what he was talking about. I didn't want any of those things he'd mentioned. He wasn't hearing me out.

He took me by the hand and we paid our bill at the bar and he drove me back to his motel room. It reminded me of childhood. The room was cold, though. At least the air conditioner was working.

We had sex that night, several times. I'd never experienced anything like it, and even after all that time since Africa, it was like we were just picking up right where we'd left off. It was otherworldly. Something that you only read about in romance novels. I'd never had anything like that except with Robert.

And against these sweeping, important backdrops. First Kenya and now the pipeline. Something about it felt cosmic. Bigger than both of us. And I was in love with him.

I had been since that first day in Africa. Even if I wasn't ready to admit it to myself until that night in a South Dakota motel on the side of the highway.

We slept with only the sheet over us. I enjoyed the way the frigid air from the window unit felt on my skin, and I enjoyed even more the feeling of his chest rising and falling against the side of my face with my hand resting in the center of it.

I closed my eyes, soaking it in. I think, even then, there was a part of me that knew it couldn't last. Not something with that much pyrotechnics. Fireworks shows are beautiful, but by dawn, you'd never even know they had happened. The sky would remain unchanged and life would go on.

I couldn't see that then, though.

I stayed awake all night, just soaking it all in. I replayed every moment of the night over and over again in my mind before the sun rose.

Without a word, when he woke, he pulled my body on top of him, and we did it again. He had eyes only for me in that moment. Those things he said felt like a distant memory. My hurt feelings must have been the result of too much alcohol flowing through my veins.

Not the result of any truth I'd heard.

He pulled me down and kissed me deeply.

"God, I'm glad I came here," he said.

"I am, too," I said, rolling over beside him.

"You're something else," he said.

"I could say the same thing about you," I said. What I wanted to tell him was that I loved him. That the distance didn't matter. We could make it work. The naivety I had floors me now. But sex and chemistry like that is intoxicating. It's rare, and to say you'd be above its influence is a flat out lie.

I'd have thrown myself in front of a semi right then for him.

He stroked my hair, playing with it as we lay there.

I could have stayed there forever, content right there in that motel room.

But eventually Robert wanted to get up. And we needed to get back to work.

I took a shower and he drove me back to the protest site. We parked and headed out to document the day. I found my eyes straying, searching for him throughout the day, but every time I found him, I never once caught him looking back at me. He was fully engrossed in the task at hand, which was capturing the moments in front of him.

I wondered if he'd burned the shape of my hands into his brain the way I had burned his into mine. I could have sketched the shape of them. The shape of his whole body. I'd have recognized his silhouette even from behind. That's how close I felt to him.

I'd never felt it before, and I've never felt it since.

SIXTEEN

WE STAYED in South Dakota until the protests were over, and even though I came away from all of it feeling heavier, the fact that I'd been with Robert again more than made up for it in my mind. I hated the fact that journalism for me came in a poor second behind Robert. But it certainly didn't come second in his priorities.

I couldn't see that, though. And I was willing to do anything to keep him.

He was traveling to Arizona after that. I decided to follow him, hoping to catch a story of my own on the way. It was the first time I'd ever traveled like that. Without a plan or without a story in mind. It felt chaotic, but it was exhilarating, too.

He'd been hesitant when I'd told him I wanted to go with him. I brushed it aside, waving away his concerns.

"I don't want you to get hurt, Jo," he said.

"I'm a big girl. I can worry about myself," I told him with a smile.

He looked at me skeptically, though. And there was a sick part of me that thought maybe, if he's afraid of me getting hurt, it means he cares about me even if he doesn't know it yet. My thoughts were in a toxic spiral.

I didn't care about finding another story once we reached our destination. Robert wanted to take photos of a peyote ceremony in the desert. The thought that I could get a story of my own wasn't even in the forefront of my mind. All I could think about was him and the prospect of either winning him over or losing him forever. Every day felt like I was tiptoeing around a box of aged dynamite, hoping something wouldn't set it off.

It didn't matter, though. Not to me at the time. I was there with him, and I wanted to stay together as long as we could. I was still kidding myself, thinking that we could actually make it past the trip to Arizona.

The night of the ceremony, after things were over, one of the guys that had been there gave Robert something. As we were leaving, he walked over to me and whispered in my ear.

"That guy gave me ecstasy. You wanna take it?"

He smiled at me and it caught me off guard.

There'd been no drugs up to that point, and I'd never used ecstasy even though I'd been a pretty hard partier in my early twenties. I look at him, shock written on my features. I felt like a kid having to turn down drugs like they told us we would in the D.A.R.E. program.

"Don't you want to?" he asked me in the car. I'd gotten quiet.

I looked over at him and he grabbed my hand, kissing the back of it. His eyes were pleading. He wanted to have a good time, and I felt like if I said no, I was ending things right then and there. He wanted someone who was wild and didn't want to be tied down by anything. Women who wanted to be married and settle down didn't do ecstasy in motel rooms. I wanted to show him that I was what he was looking for.

"Sure," I finally said.

He squeezed my hand and drove faster the rest of the way back to the motel.

He gave me the pill once we got inside and it took about twenty minutes before I felt anything.

It kicked in for Robert at about the same time.

My heart started racing and I felt hot. I stripped out of my shirt and my jeans, trying to get comfortable. I turned the air down to sixty degrees. We sat on the bed and Robert kissed me. He wanted to touch me all over and I just felt horrible.

I thought I was going to throw up and I couldn't sit still. I was so thirsty. I wondered how strong the pills were.

"Do you know what dosage these are?" I asked Robert, half-panicked. I felt like I was just getting hotter and thirstier. My heart rate hadn't slowed down and he was getting irritated with me.

"Just come lay down," Robert said. "You're fine. It's fine, Jo. Just enjoy it."

"I'm *not* enjoying it," I said definitively.

"What's the matter?" Robert asked.

I crumpled down on the floor, my chest hurting. I thought I was having a heart attack. It felt like someone was squeezing my heart with a fist. The only other time I'd felt it was right before my mother had died. I didn't know what I was going to do, even though we'd never had a good relationship. My dad had been gone for a long time at that point. If she died, as difficult as she was, it meant that I was really alone in the world. And I panicked at the thought.

"Jo, it's okay," Robert said from the bed.

I rocked back and forth, thinking I was about to die.

"I don't feel good," I told him.

The panic attack intensified, and my mind broke open.

That's the only way I know to describe it. In that moment, a flood of memories came to me, and they were all from the night that Jordan's mom was abducted.

I could see the police lights at the campground. I could see Jordan's face illuminated by them with tears streaking down her face. We were both scared. My mom had been drunk when the police had called her, but she was coming to get us anyway.

I wanted my dad.

I wanted him because I always felt like he could protect me. I think that was the first time he ever really, truly disappointed me. This was before cell phones, so when he went to the bar, he was gone for the night. I was angry, imagining myself screaming at him when he drug in that night, drunker than a skunk.

My mom would probably yell at him for me.

And he'd probably take off again.

I was running through the woods. Jordan was right on my heels.

I didn't remember this. This was something that had never come to the forefront of my mind.

We saw him.

We saw him closing the tailgate of his truck. Her mom's bare foot was hanging out. She'd lost her shoe. I remember the bare sole of her foot in the moonlight. Jordan ran towards her mother and I grabbed her by the arm, pulling her back into the bushes. I covered her mouth and told her to be quiet.

I should have done something different. I should have been brave and ran out of the woods just like Jordan wanted to. Maybe we could have saved her mom.

But something told me that if we left our hiding place, neither of us would ever be seen again.

In that moment, another part of the memory became crystal clear.

There was someone else in the truck.

And just then, he turned around and looked at us.

And everything went black.

I was screaming for help. Screaming for someone to dial 911.

Robert was telling me everything was okay. Telling me I needed to relax. He got me water and half-heartedly patted my back. I could tell he was scared but I didn't care. I couldn't get ahold of myself. I screamed until there was a knock at the door.

The police had come. Someone had called them.

I was numb, unsure of what I'd unlocked in my mind but certain that it had broken me.

I had kept Jordan from trying to save her mother. And then I had seen Nathan Kelly, and whatever happened after that I had no memory of.

My heart was still racing and my adrenaline was spent.

Robert told the police I was having a panic attack and he couldn't get me to calm down. EMTs came. They took me to the closest hospital with a psych ward, and Robert came with me.

"It's for the best," he said, holding my hand as I signed the paperwork for admission.

It wouldn't have happened without the ecstasy. I knew that.

I couldn't bring myself to tell him that. Even then, I didn't want to upset him. I'd had a panic attack so severe that the police were called on us, and I still thought there was a chance he would stay. He'd been telling me for two weeks that he was a leaver.

I should have taken him at his word.

I tried to call him from the ward one afternoon and the number had been disconnected.

He didn't want to hear from me ever again.

He made that very clear.

He took me to my lowest point and left me there like garbage tossed beside the road.

He unlocked a memory that haunted me every night I was in that hospital. When I got out, I went home to Oklahoma. Home to my mother's house. I stayed there. I got a therapist. And then I got Ghost.

I was diagnosed with bipolar disorder type 1 and severe anxiety. I never told my therapist what I had seen during my panic attack. What memories had come to me.

I kept that locked away deep.

And I vowed then that I'd do anything I could to make things right for Jordan, or at least honor the memory of her mother somehow. And that's when I started turning my focus to crime, and eventually to Nathan Kelly himself.

I never told him that I was there the night he abducted Jordan's mother.

So many times I wanted to tell him that. To tell him that it was all for her and that he might have taken her mother but he could never take her memory. But I knew how that would go. Nathan Kelly was a killer. He was vicious. He would laugh in my face and I would be left sobbing, raging against him. His self-satisfaction was so hard to sit there and take.

I could recall the shape of him in the darkness. The way he'd turned as soon as he heard us stirring in the bushes. If I'd let Jordan run out there, there's no telling what would have happened. But I didn't. I should have. And I should have run after her. Screamed for help. Someone would have heard us. And even if they didn't and he killed both of us, at least Jordan would never have to be without her mother and I wouldn't have to live with the memory of that night and the memories of watching my best friend become a shell of a person.

I tried to contact Robert one more time when I got out.

I emailed him.

He never answered me.

Sometimes I would look him up on social media. Just to see how he was doing. I wanted to reach out to him and tell him how great I was doing. But it was a lie.

I wasn't doing well for a really long time.

Ghost brought me back to life and back to myself.

He made it bearable to go in public again. I could grocery shop for myself once more. I could go get dinner or a beer in town without constantly looking over my shoulder. Ghost did those things for me. He kept distance between me and other people when I waited in line, walking constant circles around me or lying down behind me to create space. He pawed at my leg when someone was approaching from behind.

I wanted so badly to let Robert know how I felt about what he'd done, but I never did. How pathetic would it be to reach out only to berate him and then insist how well I was doing when I needed a dog to help me make it through each day. I'd done some freelance jobs, but nothing of any significance.

It was after things started to reach an even keel that I decided to write the book on Nathan Kelly.

One night, I was watching television, Ghost laying on my legs in my mother's trailer on that old floral couch, when there was a news story about him. And I knew right then that I was the person to write it. I had a unique perspective and I wouldn't go easy on him. There would be nothing sympathetic about it and I would advocate for the victims.

I would do whatever I could to help something like what he did to Jordan's mother not happen ever again.

Including sitting across from Nathan Kelly in a maximum security prison, listening to that narcissist recount his crimes, one by one.

SEVENTEEN

I TRAVELED to Colorado within a month. Making the arrangements was easier than I thought it'd be. I spent that month researching everything I could about forensic psychology and reaching out to experts that might have guidance for me on my quest. Most of them didn't write back, and the ones that did basically told me I was in way over my head here. I needed to leave it to the professionals.

But I knew this story needed to be told.

And I knew I was the right person to tell it.

The first day I went to the maximum security prison, it was a gorgeous day outside. Inside the prison, fluorescent lights stood in for actual daylight. None of the cells had windows. There was barbed wire and razor wire surrounding the place and guards ready to pick any escapees off with rifles.

Inside, it felt heavy. Like the bad energy of the things

all the people there had done was hanging in the air. After checking in, and being eyed very skeptically by several guards, one of the guards walked me down to the area where prisoners received visitors.

Kelly had known I was coming, and he was eagerly awaiting the chance to tell his story, he told me. To get his side of things down on paper for the record.

Walking down the hallway leading to the visitors' area was intimidating. There were people in cells on one side, all of them pressing their faces against the bars of their cells, some of them whistling and others making lewd remarks. I did my best to keep my attention focused forward. The guard shouted at a couple of the more unruly inmates. But the worst was when I got to the end.

Right as I walked by, an inmate reached his hand out and grazed my arm, almost touching my breast. I jumped to the side and let out a little yelp.

"Get your hands back in your cell, Dawson," the guard said. "Sorry about that." He turned to me. "You alright?"

"I'm fine," I said, but I gathered my cardigan tighter around me, feeling suddenly exposed and vulnerable. I needed to remember that I was in a maximum security prison. This wasn't like the usual interviews I did. Most of the people that I had interviewed up to that point weren't dangerous. Even when I started covering crime, I was talking to victims. Never to killers or criminals.

The guard walked me into a room with bars on the outside. There were tables around the room, but it wasn't very big. I sat down and got my notebook out, and I waited.

My stomach was in knots at the thought of seeing Nathan Kelly up close. I knew he was the man I'd seen in the parking lot that night. He was the one who took Jordan's mother. And within a few moments, the door opened and there he was.

Nathan Kelly was shorter than I remembered. Something that often happens when you're recalling an adult from your childhood. Maybe it was the shadows or just the fact that he had my friend's mom. He seemed so much bigger and much, much scarier.

He smiled at me right away when he came in the room.

"Josephine Larson," he said, even before the guard had stepped out and shut the door. The guard handcuffed him to the center of the table, something that was of little comfort to me. Part of me wanted the guard to stay, but I knew Kelly wouldn't talk with him there. Especially not if there was anything incriminating he might tell me. I wanted to get whatever information I could from him. Anything that would help investigators understand these guys more. Or keep potential victims safe.

"That's me," I told him, extending a hand.

He took it, his palm dry and warm. His handshake was firm. The kind an honest man might have. It wasn't anything like I'd imagined. I'd thought it might be weak and fish-like, his palm sweaty and clammy. But he shook hands like all the men I'd known in my life. My dad, my grandpa, my high school English teacher who shook my hand when I graduated.

It occurred to me then that Nathan Kelly wasn't some remarkable evil creature that you'd see coming a mile away. At first glance, he seemed like anyone else. You wouldn't sense the darkness in him until it was too late.

He had a slimy way about him, though. He leaned forward across the table.

"What's a pretty girl like you doin' out here in a place like this?" Kelly asked me.

I'd considered that he might ask something like that. And I'd prepared.

"Dark fascination with serial killers," I told him with a smile. "I'm writing a book, and I think you'd make a great subject. I'd like to understand your motivations. How your mind works."

He narrowed his eyes. He wasn't falling for that so easily.

"You sure gotta have a better reason than that. Dark fascination? Can't you watch YouTube?"

"I've watched plenty of YouTube. It's not like meeting someone in person," I said, feeling a little uneasy with how quickly he attacked my motives.

"I suppose that's true. But what the hell could I tell you that hasn't been said before? You think I know why I do this shit? If I knew, I probably wouldn't do it, would I?" Kelly gave me a look that reminded me of a parent making a point to their child.

He had to have been in his late thirties or early forties when I'd seen him last.

Now, he was on the verge of fifty or sixty. One of the things that the press ran with when he was caught was how handsome he was.

I could see their point, sitting across from him.

If you were just looking at a picture of the guy, you might swipe right on Tinder. But if he was right in front of you, the creepiness just radiated out of every pore on his body. I felt uncomfortable in my own skin in front of him, suddenly wishing there wasn't a shred of skin showing. I didn't want his eyes roving down my neck like they were.

I brought a hand to my throat. He reacted.

"You don't like it when I look at you like that?" he asked.

I'd never been around someone who asked such disarming questions and spoke the truth like Kelly. Or at least the truth that served him. He had no filter for what was appropriate, and I'm guessing he had no feeling for it either.

"No, it's not that," I said, clearing my throat. I didn't know how to answer the question. Being honest would tell him he'd gotten to me. I knew that was a possibility when I signed up to do this.

"They try to wear you down," one expert said who didn't immediately tell me I was in no position to go see Nathan Kelly face to face.

"You can be honest with me, Josephine," he said, using my name.

It reminded me of a sales technique. Something you might do if you wanted someone to spend a large amount of money. Lull them into the false sense that they see you as important and that they care about you.

"I'm fine," I said with a smile, trying to relax my posture. "I'm here to talk about you, anyway," I reminded him.

"Well, I'm an open book, honey," he said, leaning back as far as he could with his hands cuffed to the bolt at the center of the table. He crossed one leg over the other. "Ask me anything you'd like to know."

"Tell me about your life before all of this. Start wherever you'd like," I said. I pulled out my recorder. "Okay if I record?"

"Sure," he said with a polite nod.

I started it.

"Well, I guess I was like anybody else," Kelly said. "Maybe a little too obsessed with women," he speculated. "I didn't have much luck with girls when I was younger. I had my first and only girlfriend when I was twenty-six," he said. "Late bloomer, I guess you could say," he added with a smile.

"Tell me about that relationship," I said.

Kelly seemed to think about it for a moment.

"She was wonderful," he said. "Just an angel, you know? She always had food ready for me when I got home. Made sure the house was always clean. Hadn't been with a lot of other men. She never talked back to me, either. And she gave great blow jobs," he added so casually that it disarmed me once again.

Kelly paused and looked at me.

He knew he was making me uncomfortable. I had to get over that if I was going to make this work. He was unpredictable, I realized. It made me glad I'd decided to leave Ghost at the motel, safe in his crate, taking a nap.

I didn't want him in here in case something went wrong.

I decided to push back a little bit.

"Those sound like qualities someone might be looking for in the 1950s," I said with an innocent smile. "Do you prefer women to be submissive?"

"I don't like a woman that talks back, if that's what you mean," Kelly said. "You think you could get me some cigarettes?" He asked the question quickly. It was important to him, I realized. He wasn't able to wait for a better moment. It gave me leverage.

"I could probably do that," I said. "But I need you to do something for me."

"What's that darlin'?" he asked, eyeing me skeptically. There was rage just below the surface of his gaze. He didn't like being out of control. Especially when it meant that a woman had control.

"I'll keep you stocked in cigarettes if you'll share more with me about everything that happened than you have before," I said.

He narrowed his eyes, almost like he was weighing the consequences of a deal like this.

"How do you mean?" he asked with a laugh. "I already told everything there was to tell, hence I ended up here." He pointed at the room around us. "And cigarettes ain't the bargaining chip you think they are," he added with a snarl.

I'd gotten to him.

"I'll bring them tomorrow," I said. "And tomorrow you'll tell me about the first woman you killed. The entirety of the crime. Anything that you left out the first time. What could it matter, anyway? You're already here," I remarked.

He lurched forward and pounded his hands on the steel table. His eyes nearly bulged out of his head and I pushed back in my seat.

"You think you know me?" Kelly asked through gritted teeth.

I took a deep breath.

"I'd like to," I told him. Although getting to know this man was a disgusting possibility. Even so, it was my goal.

"What do you know, bitch?" Kelly spat at me. "Guard!" he yelled as he plopped back down in his chair.

The prison guard opened the giant cell and came to collect Kelly. He glanced at me, and I guess he read my emotions on my face.

"I'll be back for you," he said to me, and walked Kelly out of the room and down the hallway.

I took a deep breath and looked at my hands. They were shaking.

I hadn't accounted for how unnerving this could all be. Was I cut out for this? Could I really do this? I left the prison with those questions in mind that day.

I went back to my motel and packed my bag. I decided this had been a horrible mistake and I needed to course correct. The experts that had turned me away were right: I wasn't in any position to be interviewing an actual serial killer. And it couldn't be doing anything good for my mental health to be spending day after day with him, like I was planning on doing.

After I packed my bag, I curled up in the motel bed with Ghost. He laid his head on my thigh and snuggled with me as we watched reality TV. It was a much needed palette cleanser from the day I'd had.

I opened my phone and started scrolling through Facebook.

And that's when I saw a post Jordan had made.

It was a picture of her mother, Gloria, taken a month before she went missing, according to the caption Jordan put with it. And today, just so happened to be the anniversary of the day Gloria went missing.

I stared at my screen for a few minutes, reading the post over and over and looking at the image of the woman who had been a second mom to me as a kid.

That was all it took.

I put Ghost's harness on him and we went to the convenience store to get cigarettes.

EIGHTEEN

"HERE," I said, passing the cigarettes across the table.

Nathan Kelly restrained himself, waiting until they'd been sitting there for a few seconds before he put his hands on them. But by the way he grabbed them, I knew this was a currency I could use with him. I'd read so much about serial killers that would talk as long as they could get outside luxuries. Sometimes to the detriment of the researcher. It could cause false confessions. Anything to keep the goodies coming.

I intended to cash in on that.

"Thank you," Kelly said, clasping the cigarettes between his two palms.

"You're welcome," I said. "Tell me about the first woman you killed," I added, less as a question and more as an imperative.

"What do you wanna know about her?" Kelly asked, pulling the cellophane off the pack of cigarettes. He opened them and pressed them to his nose, inhaling deeply. "Nothin' smells better than a fresh pack of cigarettes."

"How did you choose her?" I asked.

I thought about being in that campground. Jordan and I were telling each other scary stories in our tent. Her mom had just excused herself to go to the bathroom. She told us to yell if anything went wrong. She was more concerned about something happening to us than she was about something happening to her.

"She was alone," he said. "Well, she had two little girls with her. But she left them behind and went to the bathroom. I could see her from the parking lot where I was sittin' in my truck watchin'."

I swallowed, my mouth going slightly dry.

"Why the campground?" I asked.

"Women are vulnerable there," he said. "Out in the elements, they aren't in their natural habitat. It gave me an extra advantage over them. And there was somethin' about pickin' someone off from a group that just really did it for me, you know? I get hard just thinkin' about it."

I didn't bother asking about the implication of the statement.

"Do you think that was a control thing?" I asked.

"I'm sure it was," he says. "But mainly, I just enjoyed it. I always liked huntin' when I was a kid. Huntin' people was even better. Animals get scared but it's nothin' like the look in a woman's eyes when she knows what you're gonna do to her after you get her alone."

My stomach turned at the statement. Immediately, I pictured Gloria. Were her eyes wide with terror when she faced her captor?

"How'd you keep her from alerting anyone?" I asked.

"I hit her over the head with a rock. Knocked her out cold. Then I carried her back to the truck," he said.

"She was missing for two months before her body was found," I said. "What happened in that time frame."

Kelly leaned closer to me, like he was about to tell me some kind of secret. I couldn't help but lean closer to him, hopeful that he was going to reveal something I hadn't even thought to ask about. Something that might confirm what I believed to be true.

"I did anything and everything you can imagine, honey," he said, his eyes deadlocked with mine as he clutched his precious pack of cigarettes. "I used her up nice and good and then I was gonna hunt her on my property. But she was too weak for that. It took the fun out of it. I liked it when they could still run, put up a fight. There ain't nothin' fun about shootin' fish in a barrel. So I dumped her."

The way he says it so casually is enough to make my skin crawl. Rage bubbles up inside me. He saw Gloria's ruined body as *trash* to be *dumped*. How callous and how far removed from humanity do you have to be to look at another human being that way?

I wondered in that moment if Nathan Kelly had a soul.

I wasn't even sure I believed in God or souls or any of

that. But I was sure that if they did exist, he didn't have one. He was pure evil.

"That bother you?" he asked, leaning back.

"I think it would bother anyone," I say. "But I'm not here to judge you. A court has already done that."

"They sure have," he says with a smile. "Judge said I was the worst criminal he'd ever seen."

"What else can you tell me about Gloria?" I asked, accidentally using her name. "I mean your first victim."

"Was that her name?" When he asked it, the corner of his mouth turned up. I felt a twitch near my mouth. I didn't blink. "I guess I never bothered to ask her."

"She had a daughter," I said, my jaw tight.

"Yeah, she did," he says, his voice wistful as if he's recalling the night that he kidnapped her. "Never saw the daughter. Was she pretty like her mama?"

"She was at your trial," I said.

"Guess she must not have been that pretty or I'd remember her," he said with a shrug.

I inhaled sharply, thinking about Jordan. All the loss and heartache she'd endured and was still enduring every single day. No one deserved that. And this person that had done it to her talked about it all like it was the most normal thing in the world. Like small talk you might have with a teller at the bank.

"You don't think much of your victims," I remarked. "Is that a feeling you have about women in general?"

"Women ain't nothin' but trouble," Kelly said.

"What about that first girlfriend?" I probed further. "She seemed pretty great. Wonderful, in your words."

"She was great until she wasn't," Kelly said with a dismissive gesture of his hand. "She ended up being a whore like the rest of y'all."

He made eye contact with me then that unnerved me. It was a reminder that I was alone in a room with a man whose hobby had been torturing women to death. Not once, not twice, but at least thirteen times. And those were only the ones that the police knew about.

He went on then, breaking our eye contact.

"She found someone else," he said.

"Did she cheat on you?" I asked, trying to sound sympathetic.

"No. She'd left me before she got with this guy. But he was everything I wasn't," he said. "Everything she'd been nagging me to be. The nagging was what really destroyed us," he said with a nod, like he was reassuring himself.

"Do you think things could have been different?" I asked.

"I don't," he said. "She'd gotten the idea that she deserved better. Wasn't nothin' I could do to convince her otherwise. She just got to be an uppity bitch," he said, matter-of-fact.

"And you didn't date anyone after her?" I asked.

"No," he said. "I had some trouble meeting women after that," he said. "I could just see right through y'all. All women care about is money and what they can use a man for. My mother was the same, hoppin' from relationship to relationship until she'd drained the guy of whatever he could give her."

I glanced at my recorder, making sure it was getting this. Kelly, like so many serial killers, had a deep-seated hatred of women going back to his mother. I thought immediately of Ed Kemper. Likely, the only reason Kelly hadn't made his own mother a victim was because she'd already been dead by the time he started victimizing women for his own pleasure.

"I'm sorry that was your experience," I said to him, wanting to poke at him slightly and make it clear that I didn't share the same worldview and that I was willing to challenge him on it.

"You gonna tell me women ain't like that?" Kelly asked then, an edge in his voice. "Every single one of those gals I killed got exactly what was comin' to her."

NINETEEN

GHOST and I went for walks near our motel every night after I'd get home from the prison. The whole process was becoming a lonely business, and I really didn't have anyone to call for moral support. Any time I called my dad, he'd either not answer, or find a way to get off the phone quickly. Mom was gone. Jordan and I weren't close like we used to be, and she'd specifically asked me not to talk to her about what I was doing in Colorado.

Because of that, most of my evenings were spent with Ghost as my only company alongside my memories from the day's events, which mainly contained whatever Nathan Kelly and I had talked about. I still wasn't getting what I wanted out of him.

That particular night, I thought about the last time I'd seen Robert.

And the memory that had unlocked for me.

That night, standing in the woods, grabbing Jordan

by the arm and keeping her from going after her mother. I hadn't just seen Nathan Kelly standing beside the tailgate of his truck.

There was a second person in the cab of the truck.

A man. He was wearing a baseball cap.

I had walked further than I meant to from the motel, and Ghost began to whine, alerting me to something. I felt a chill and pulled my jacket tighter around me. Sun was setting and in the distance I saw two sets of eyes. Likely coyotes.

"Come on, baby. Let's go," I said to Ghost.

He turned around eagerly and we started back for the motel. I had no doubt that Ghost would go after anyone or anything that tried to hurt me, but I had zero desire to see that in action and risk him getting hurt.

We got back to the motel and I ate gas station snacks for dinner.

I couldn't get the image of the second man out of my head.

The police interviewed both me and Jordan when we were kids about what we'd seen. I told the officer that talked to us about the second man, but nothing ever came of it. When I started doing my research for the book, there was no evidence of the report I gave. And no where else was something like that documented.

There were things about some of Nathan Kelly's crimes, though, that made me wonder if I'd made it up. Nathan Kelly's DNA was found with all the victims.

There was zero evidence that anyone but Nathan Kelly raped those women.

It was something that kept me up sometimes. Tonight included.

I'd thought about just straight up asking him about it. I brought up the possibility that there might have been someone working with him to my editor. She wasn't crazy about suggesting something like that without evidence. She asked me why I thought that was a possibility. I didn't have the courage to tell her what I'd seen when I was a kid.

In the book, I left that part out. I shared that Jordan and I had seen Kelly. I didn't share that there had been another man. It was too bold a claim to make without solid proof.

And there was nothing resembling that at any point.

I thought about serial killers like Dean Corll and Elmer Wayne Henley. Maybe Nathan Kelly had an accomplice. Maybe someone that helped him find victims. Helped him with disposing of the bodies. What would be in it for him, though?

It wasn't the same dynamic that Corll and Henley had.

This was something else.

But I knew what I'd seen. Or at least I thought I did.

I curled up on the bed with Ghost and turned on the television. I'd gotten a little streaming device to plug into the motel TV and I navigated to a documentary about serial killers. It was a wide, sweeping show about several men and their crimes. I looked for similarities with Nathan Kelly.

I kept trying to come up with a way that I could ask him about the other man.

I knew that Kelly wasn't going to offer that up, and there was every chance—if there was any truth to it—that Kelly would completely shut down after I brought it up.

I couldn't ask him yet. I needed to gain his trust first, if that was possible.

I pulled Ghost closer to me and he laid his front leg across my leg and rested his head on my thigh. He sighed with deep contentment. I stoked his head and he cut his eyes up at me, checking in with me like he did frequently.

"What are we doing?" I asked Ghost.

He looked up at me, raising his head.

"Everything's okay," I assured him, stroking his head. "I think I've just lost my mind."

Ghost sighed again and laid his head on my leg.

I continued to watch the documentary and think about Kelly, wondering what he was thinking about me. If he was actively deceiving me. I had no doubt that he would if he needed to. After the documentary finished, I took Ghost and we went across the parking lot to the gas station. I grabbed a Dr. Pepper for Kelly. In an interview I'd read with him, he mentioned it was his favorite.

I grabbed a candybar, too, though I wasn't sure it was his favorite. But who would turn one of those down if they were in prison? I imagine they weren't that easy to come by behind bars. And I knew that kind of currency might be a way to build trust. I needed Kelly to think I cared about him.

I needed him to think I was someone he could use or manipulate for whatever purpose he saw fit. Maybe doing these interviews with me was just a form of entertainment for him. He was facing the rest of his life in prison. It was nothing to him to spend this time with me. Otherwise, he'd just be staring at a cinderblock wall.

However he looked at me, I needed to begin winning his trust. And I thought this was a good start.

TWENTY

HE EAGERLY ACCEPTED my gifts over the next few days. I even asked him if he had preferences. It turned out PayDay's were his favorite. Dr. Pepper had been spot on, though. I brought him one of each every day. So long as Kelly kept entertaining my presence, the treats would keep coming. It was so simple and basic, like conditioning an animal. I wondered if there was any possibility that Kelly didn't see that.

But he seemed to enjoy it. And he started to talk more casually with me. He began to open up, talking more about his childhood and early adulthood. He softened with me slightly, realizing that I wasn't going anywhere any time soon. And I think he realized that I did have a genuine interest in him and his life.

What he didn't know was that I just wanted him to slip up. To mention some small detail that could confirm what I'd seen as a kid.

One night in the motel, I was snuggling with Ghost, and trying to put out of my mind the grisly description Kelly had given me of one of his crimes earlier in the day when I had an idea.

I was going to tell him that I'd been there the night Gloria White went missing.

That I'd been a kid. I'd been at the campground that night.

It's something that I'd told myself I shouldn't share. That it was far too vulnerable of a detail to share with someone like Kelly. He would immediately twist it into something that he could use against me.

But there was also the possibility he would be caught off guard by it. Maybe I needed to wait another week.

I decided I would wait. And we continued on in that fashion for the next week. And the week after that. And the week after that. Time passed quickly and before I knew it, I'd been spending every afternoon for a month with Nathan Kelly, the Heartland Hunter. I had plenty of information for my book, but what I really wanted was the detail that would allow me to confirm he hadn't acted alone.

It was halfway into the third month of interviewing him that I finally took my chance.

Kelly was telling me a story about something that had happened to him after he'd killed his second victim. He was sharing with me the thrill of hunting the girl. It was enough to turn an uninitiated person's stomach. It bothered me how desensitized I was becoming to his lengthy descriptions.

I would shower at night, turning the water as hot as possible, trying to wash his words out of my ears. I would pull Ghost close, listening to the sound of his breathing at night, using it to ground myself.

My thoughts drifted to that as Kelly spoke. I thought about how I'd take a shower later and take Ghost for a walk. Then we'd have dinner and snuggle. Sometimes the thoughts of those small comforts were what got me through especially intense days like this one.

When he finished talking, I realized that I hadn't really been listening all that much. My heart rate had picked up, thinking about asking the question that I'd come to Colorado to ask.

He paused, taking a sip of his Dr. Pepper.

"You in there, Joey?" Kelly asked.

It snapped me right back to reality. The name was one only my father used with me. Kelly smirked when it got my attention.

"Don't call me that," I said quickly.

"Oh, sorry. I didn't know it was a sore spot," he said. But the look on his face clearly told me that he was tucking that bit of information away for a rainy day to use against me when it most served him.

"I want to ask you something," I said.

"Well, shoot," he said, casual as ever.

"Well, I guess I need to tell you something first," I said.

This seemed to get his attention, the idea that I could have anything to share with him.

"Do you remember the night you kidnapped your first victim?"

It was a stupid question. Kelly had recounted it to me more than twice, waxing poetic about the whole thing.

"Of course," Kelly said with a solemness. Almost like the experience had been holy for him.

It made my skin crawl.

I swallowed hard.

"I was there that night," I said.

It was a risk. I knew that.

Kelly's face was impenetrable for a moment, his eyes locked on mine. He rubbed the sides of his face.

"Were you? Now, that's interesting," he said, seeming to really like the idea of this.

"I was," I said. "I saw you."

He looked at me then like he was trying to calculate where I was going with this.

I leaned across the table, clasping my hands in front of me.

"Who was the other man?" I whispered.

Kelly gave me a steely look as a smile slowly crept up at the corners of his mouth. He leaned forward across the table, getting closer to me than he'd ever been before. I could smell his breath, sour and stale. I stood my ground, continuing to lean forward, letting him know that I wasn't going anywhere. I demanded an answer to the question. It might be my only opportunity.

He licked his lips and then he spoke in a low voice that I still hear sometimes when I can't sleep.

"Wouldn't you like to know, Joey?"

My mask of fierceness faltered at the mention of the nickname again. He was doing it to disarm me, and it was working.

I inhaled sharply through my nose.

"Who was he?" I pressed.

Kelly leaned back.

"I think we're done here for today," he said simply.

He called for the guard, who came quickly to collect him. And he winked at me as he rounded the corner, passing out of sight.

I inhaled deeply.

It was true.

I knew he wouldn't have responded that way if it wasn't.

It was confirmation of what I'd seen. I didn't imagine it. And I wasn't losing my mind.

I glanced over at the bars on the side of the room.

And just then, I heard Nathan Kelly.

He was whistling.

TWENTY-ONE

I WAS careful going forward and I didn't bring it up again for months.

I stayed in Colorado for the better part of a year as I drafted the book. I put our conversations in it. I called my editor and told her what he'd said about the other man. She told me it still wasn't enough. That there was no evidence, and it could be dangerous to claim such a thing. It could be Kelly wanting to shift the blame to someone else if he did admit to it. And besides, the way it had gone down, it was as though I'd suggested the idea to him.

I called the police, too, but they dismissed me. They weren't impressed by the fact that I didn't have any real credentials to be interviewing a serial killer. And they took it the same way my editor did, cautioning me against the possibility of putting ideas in Nathan Kelly's head.

I hung up, frustrated, both times.

I knew what I'd seen.

The memory was clear. The second man had been sitting in the passenger seat of the truck. He wore a baseball cap and his head was turned slightly to the side. Not far enough to see his profile, but more than enough to see the bill of the cap.

The image of Gloria's bare foot came back to me then.

I knew this was true. The look in Kelly's eyes said as much. He *knew* I'd seen them both.

Our interviews continued, me dancing around that subject, until one day, he brought Gloria up.

"Whatever happened to that woman's daughter?" he asked.

"Gloria White's daughter?" I asked, irritated that after all this time he hadn't bothered to learn a single victim's name. To him, they were just replaceable objects with heartbeats. Toys for him to use and dispose of.

"Yeah, that one," he said.

"She grew up. Had a daughter of her own," I said.

"Was she okay?" he asked.

"No. She wasn't," I said, immediately regretting it because of the look on Kelly's face.

"It messed her up good for me to kill her mama, huh?"

"It would be traumatic for anyone," I said, wanting to take the focus off Jordan. "I imagine you had much the same effect on other victims' family members."

"I wonder what it was like for her," Kelly said, referencing Jordan. I bristled. "I wonder if she dreams about me. Did she see me that night?"

The question sent a shiver through me.

I nodded, unable to speak.

"So, she saw this other man, too?" he probed.

"No," I said.

"So, it was just you who saw this 'other man'?"

The insinuation was clear.

"Where's your dog?" Kelly asked. "You mentioned him one time. Ghost, I think his name was."

I regretted it instantly. I'd mentioned him in a conversation with the guard. I hadn't thought Kelly had heard.

"Service dog, isn't he? But like a special kind. For crazy people, right? People who get scared easy and can't handle their emotions," he went on.

I inhaled deeply, telling myself not to let him get to me.

It wasn't working, though. It was all too personal, preying on my insecurities.

"Who would believe anything you had to say?" he asked quietly, leaning across the table. "Some wannabe psychologist with some mental illness and a dog that has to go everywhere with her."

He narrowed his eyes.

"You may know what you saw, but ain't no one ever gonna believe you, Joey."

I swallow, a tear nearly escaping down my cheek.

"Ain't no one gonna believe you just like they didn't when you were a kid."

He adds the last with a savage smile. The smile of someone that knows he's getting away with something. And then he called for the guard.

***

SOME DAYS with Kelly were easy. Other days, like that day, were horrible.

I went back to the motel feeling like I'd returned from battle, defeated. I licked my wounds and cried. And then I did the only thing I could. I called my editor again. I told her what he'd said.

"He's messing with you, Josephine," she said. "That's all this is. He's gotten under your skin and it's working."

"This isn't that," I insisted. "You should have seen his eyes when he said it. I know there was another man. Someone that helped him."

"Why would he protect someone if it could get his sentence lessened if he ratted them out?" she asked.

It was a point I hadn't thought about, and her bringing it up made me feel like an idiot.

It felt like being a thirteen-year-old kid again. No one believed me.

No one except Nathan Kelly.

I thought about what my editor had said. Why would Kelly protect anyone?

But it was clear I was onto something. The way Kelly had reacted wasn't nothing. It was something. It was clear that he knew something he wasn't admitting to.

Who was he protecting?

Why?

I left Colorado with those questions, and I wasn't sure I'd ever get answers.

I thought maybe this would just be a secret that I shared with Nathan Kelly. The thought was enough to turn my stomach.

That was until I arrived in Alaska.

That gave me hope.

TWENTY-TWO

"HOLY SHIT," Parker says.

He stares at me and then leans onto the table with his elbows. He clasps his fist and rests it in front of his mouth like he's trying to think of the right response. It's the first time I've shared my theory with someone in a long time.

"Every time I tried to bring it up, I got shot down," I tell him.

"You really think he's got a partner?" Parker asks.

"I know what I saw that night," I say. I stare at Parker hard, wondering if he's doubting my story.

"I believe you," he says, looking directly into my eyes.

"The neon yellow zip ties," I say. "No one but someone who had inside information about Kelly would know that detail."

"You're right," Parker says.

"We need to tell Wilson," I tell him.

"Wait," Parker says as I try to scoot out of the booth, closing my laptop.

"What?" I ask sharply. I get the impression he doesn't want to go to his superior with this idea. "You said you believe me."

"I do believe you," Parker says, hand still on my arm. I slide back into the booth. "I just don't know how well Wilson will receive this."

I relax into my seat.

"So, what do you propose we do?" I ask.

Parker smiles.

"We wait," he says. Before I can voice my protest, he raises a hand. "I know you don't want to wait. You've waited a long time. But we need to be smart about this or Wilson will kick you out."

I know he's right. And Wilson would be well within his rights to do so. I can only imagine how he would interpret me coming in with this theory seemingly out of the blue. Especially since it never made it into the book.

It wouldn't go over well. I realize that.

"I know you're right," I say with a sigh. I rub my hands over my face.

"You have any idea who this other person might be?" Parker asks.

"Whoever it is, Kelly has some interest in protecting him," I say.

"That or he's afraid of him," Parker suggests.

I half-laugh.

The thought that Nathan Kelly would be afraid of

anyone is hard to fathom. The guy is a walking night-mare. Who would he be scared of?

"Or maybe he wants to take all the credit for it," Parker muses. "By naming an accomplice, it kind of diminishes his star."

"I hadn't thought of that," I admit.

"There are a lot of possibilities there for why he wouldn't want to name this person. But I'm guessing it's either fear or pride," Parker says. "A guy like that knows there's no way he'll ever see the outside world again. There's no incentive for him to admit he had someone help him. Maybe he's afraid of how other inmates will react if he didn't play as large a role in the murders as he makes it out that he did."

Parker says this with a shrug.

"That's a possibility," I say, rolling it over in my mind, slowly like meat on a spit.

The thought that Kelly could be afraid comes back to me. The idea is interesting. I wonder what the hell kind of boogeyman would scare a monster like Kelly.

"So, what have we got?" Parker asks, breaking me out of my trance.

"Well, we know that this guy is using the same m.o. as Kelly," I say. "Same torture. Same hunting grounds. Same neon yellow zip ties. It's down to a T. This guy could probably pass a test about Kelly that Kelly couldn't pass himself."

"What if the guy you saw wasn't an accomplice?" Parker asks.

I look at him strangely. The thought isn't one I've entertained much.

"What if he was another victim? Or someone that Kelly was using for something else. Like a guy who just happened to be in the way."

"I don't think so," I say. "Kelly was way too casual when he was at the tailgate of that truck. And so was the guy in the cab. He didn't seem frantic to get out of there. It was more like he was keeping an eye out."

"I'm just trying to go over everything," Parker says. He leans forward across the table. "I believe you. You know that right? I'm on your team here."

I'm taken aback by the way he looks at me. It's sincere. Like he really cares about me. About proving that there was a second person. It's with the same intensity that he approaches everything. I'm not expecting it.

"Thank you," I say quietly. "But why? No one ever has before."

"I'm pretty good at telling when people are telling the truth. Comes with the territory, I guess you could say," he adds with a smile. "You strike me as a genuine person. And you don't seem crazy."

"Even with my little friend under the table?" I half-joke, Nathan Kelly's words fresh on my mind about my mental health. I reach down and Ghost brings his wet nose up to touch my palm.

"Having trauma doesn't make you crazy, Josephine," Parker says. "If it did, every last person on earth would be a raving lunatic."

"Well, you certainly seem well-adjusted," I say.

"Do I come off that way?" Parker says with a laugh. "Glad to see it's working."

"Share something with me that will keep me from getting back to the hotel with a vulnerability hangover," I tell him.

I'm half-joking, but I hope he takes me up on it. His smile fades and he looks into my eyes. The air between us gets heavier. And then he speaks.

"My brother was murdered," he says.

I'm shocked by the sentence.

"I'm sorry," I say, my words barely a whisper.

"Don't be," he says. "It was a long time ago, and it's not your fault." He gives me a sad smile. "But it was a hugely formative event for me," he admits. "I was fourteen. He was twenty. He got shot in the parking lot of his apartment complex. A stray bullet. Some other altercation was happening. Domestic. The guy pulled his gun and shot. The bullet ricocheted and hit my brother right in the heart." Parker jabs his chest on the left side. "He didn't stand a chance. Dead before anyone realized what had happened."

I'm silent, unsure of what to say. Even when you've seen the dark, it doesn't make you any better at giving another person solace because they've seen it, too. And I've learned over the years that a silent presence is better than hollow words that don't mean anything and generally leave the bereaved feeling worse, not better.

"It's why I wanted to be an FBI agent. I kept out of

trouble, got good grades, went to college and majored in criminal justice. Kept my nose clean. Made it into the Academy. I just wanted to make a difference. I'm older now, a little separated from the naive kid that I was," he says with a smile. "I know how the system works, and it's not perfect. But I try to make a difference where I can."

I hesitate before speaking.

"This would make a big difference. If we could bring this guy down."

Parker's smile is replaced by seriousness. He leans forward.

"I know. And I want us to catch him, Josephine. I want us to make that difference."

TWENTY-THREE

"BEFORE YOU DO ANYTHING ELSE, I think it would be good for you to get a solid night of sleep," Parker says after we've been sitting in the bar talking until sundown.

"Ghost could probably use some downtime," I say, stroking him under the table.

"He really hasn't gotten much of a break, has he?" Parker asks. He glances under the table.

"He hasn't," I say. "I'm working him pretty hard. But he's a tough guy," I say. "I don't think he'd say no to a long nap, though." I add the last with a little smile. It's not just Ghost that's tired. I feel like I'm running on fumes. I haven't really gotten any opportunity to rest since I got here.

"Well, let's go back to the hotel. Call it a night. Start fresh in the morning," Parker says. "Shall we?"

"Yeah, let's go," I say.

Parker pays the tab and we walk with Ghost back across the street. It's almost dark outside and I'm ready to take a shower and crawl into bed. I want Ghost's head on my leg, reminding me that I'm here now. That I'm safe.

Parker, Ghost, and I get to the elevator. As I turn and face the doors, I see the two girls from the other night. The ones that were planning on going camping.

I feel a twinge of relief when I see them both. I'm glad that they're still here. That they didn't go camping. Maybe my words swayed them. I hope they did. Or that someone's did. Maybe it's the heavy FBI presence in the hotel. Surely, they've noticed. The guys in the suits get stared at when they travel in packs to their rental cars.

Parker is mostly with me, which is to say, by himself. He doesn't stick out as badly. Though I imagine we don't look like we go together. Him constantly dressed in a sharp suit and me usually in a t-shirt and jeans.

Parker waves at me from down the hall as I step into my room. It reminds me of how I would wait for Jordan to get inside her house and shut the door before I would drive off when we were teenagers. Even then, I felt a responsibility to protect her that went beyond what had happened to her as a kid. I did it because she was a girl. And the idea of losing her was unfathomable to me then.

Now, I have lost her.

The darkness swallowed her up. After her daughter was born, it brought her back halfway. But she's still inhabiting a liminal space between living and dying. I think if Shay hadn't been born, Jordan wouldn't be here anymore.

I slip into the hotel room with Ghost and switch on the light. I lock the door behind me in all the ways that I can.

Now that I've shared my thoughts with Parker, it feels real.

It feels as real as the day that Nathan Kelly looked in my eyes and confirmed my suspicion.

I know that Kelly is locked up in Colorado, but I feel him crawling all over me. Like he's here next to me, his sour breath in my ear.

I bend down and pet Ghost, taking off his harness. He shakes his whole body, knowing he's not on duty as soon as that thing is off. He's free to be a regular dog. He jumps up on the bed and nuzzles his head against the covers, side to side, at the head of the bed.

"What are you doing?" I ask him.

He whips his head around, a wild look in his eyes. I laugh.

"I'm going to take a shower," I tell him.

I make it a habit to talk to him. For so long he's been my only major companion. Talking to Parker, even if it's about Kelly, has been welcome. Ever since Robert left me in South Dakota, I haven't really opened up to anyone. Telling Parker what I really believe about Nathan Kelly and the second man in the truck was the most I've let anyone in for years.

And Parker met my vulnerability with his own.

It's something Robert could never do.

Everything was a performance for him.

I forbid myself from thinking about him tonight and go turn on the shower.

After I wash my hair, I stand under the shower head with the water as hot as it'll go, reminding myself not to let my mind wander. I don't want another situation like the other morning. Parker coming into my room, thinking I'm dead.

I get out of the shower and put my hair in a towel. I change into my pajamas and take Ghost for a quick walk to relieve himself. He does his business and we go back to our room. I crawl in bed and he snuggles up beside me, but I can't fall asleep.

As tired as I am, I'm thrilled by the possibility that Parker is taking me seriously about this.

It's the first time that anyone's believed me when I've talked about the guy in the truck. I don't think it's hit me until now what an emotional thing it is. Tears sneak down my face as I pet Ghost and we watch an HGTV show. I don't want to admit to myself how touched I am.

In another life, I could see myself being friends with someone like Parker.

He seems like a genuine person, just as he described me. But I don't know him that well. Or at all, really. Everything I've seen of him so far could be carefully curated.

Isn't that what we all do?

I stroke Ghost's fur.

Life is much less complicated when you only worry about your dog. I never wonder what Ghost's ulterior motives are. He just loves me, and his job is to keep me healthy and safe. He's outstanding at that, and he's affectionate, playful, and smart. He's better than most friends I've had in my life.

I'm pretty content with him as my only company.

But the kindness Parker showed me today makes me wonder what it might be like to connect with another human being again. Someone that I could call a friend. I'm not even sure that I remember what it's like to be a decent friend to someone. I've been on my own for so long.

This afternoon, even though it was work, felt like a little taste of that.

What it might be like to have a friend.

Am I that hard up for a connection with another person?

It's a bleak thought.

I stay up late into the night, watching episode after episode about homes being renovated, flipped, sold, bought, and all the rest. By 3:00am, I feel like I could pass a test to become either a carpenter or a realtor.

Ghost whines slightly and sits up, stretching his head far up into the air and extending his neck. He makes a funny little noise and shivers with a yawn. He whimpers again and looks at me.

"You need to go outside?" I ask.

He gives me a tiny little yelp letting me know I've nailed it.

"Come on," I say, crawling out of bed. I get my shoes and slip them on. I hook Ghost up to his leash and we head downstairs.

When the elevator on the lobby floor opens, I see the two girls from the other night at the check-in desk. They seem to be arguing a little bit.

"I'm sick of staying here. It's not what we came up here to do," one of the girls says.

The other seems hesitant.

"I just don't know if it's a good idea."

"Come on," the other girl says. She signs a receipt on the desk and hands it to the girl on the other side. She turns and heads for the main lobby door. Both of them are wearing hiking backpacks. I feel a knot in my stomach.

Surely they're not leaving in the middle of the night to go camping. I would imagine they're driving to another town first. I can't imagine they'd camp here after everything that's been going on.

I walk out behind them and take Ghost over to some grass beside the hotel. He makes quick work of it and then he's ready to go back inside and sleep some more.

Back at the room, I still can't sleep.

I'm so tired. It should be easy to fall asleep.

I wonder if Parker is awake right now.

I think about going to wake him up. But why? To tell him I can't sleep?

It's another moment that's a reminder that maybe I do need a friend. Someone I could text right now. Someone I could vent to. Share things with. Not be judged by.

Isn't that what everyone wants?

I sigh and kick my shoes off. I take Ghost's leash and hang it on the back of the chair in the room. We crawl back in bed and I change the channel to something else.

I pull the covers over my head and feel my dog place his head on my leg.

And then I do my best to fall asleep, praying that I don't dream of Nathan Kelly.

TWENTY-FOUR

I WAKE up and grab my cell phone, having the distinct feeling that I've slept in too late.

When I see the time, I realize I'm right. It's almost noon.

I throw myself out of bed and get ready quickly. I harness Ghost up and then we walk down the hall to Parker's room. I knock on the door, but he doesn't answer. I pound harder and call his name.

"Parker!" I shout.

Finally, I hear him stirring inside. And then he comes to the door.

When he opens it, he looks entirely different than I'm used to seeing him. The man that's almost in a buttoned up suit is wearing flannel pajamas and a white t-shirt. His hair is sticking up and he's currently on the phone.

He waves for me to come on in, holding the door open for me. I slip under his arm and into the room with

Ghost. I take a seat at the desk and Parker paces, waiting for something on the other end.

I stare at him as he paces. Finally, he stops and I hear the sound of a voice on the other end.

"Yes, I'm here," Parker says.

The voice on the other end says something else.

"You're sure?" he asks.

There's an affirmative noise.

"Thank you," he says. "That's good to know. That's really helpful, actually. 'Bye."

He hangs up the phone and looks at me.

"You're not going to believe this," he says.

"What's up?" I ask.

Parker smiles.

"I did some digging. I've been on the phone all morning—I told them I had a lead—and I got a lead alright," he says. "I found out that on two of the bodies that turned up on the side of the road during the years that Nathan Kelly was active had a second DNA profile on them. Another person—a man—had been with them shortly before the time of their deaths."

My eyes widen in the dark hotel room.

"There *was* another man," Parker confirms.

A little laugh escapes me.

"Wait, why would this just come up now?" I ask.

"A connection I have in OKC told me that the cops in 2003 concluded that the second DNA profile was the result of a connection they had before Nathan Kelly. What it sounds like is they were so eager to put the case to rest that they didn't want to chase down the second profile. The only catch is that the extra DNA profile on the two women matches. It was the same man. What are the odds of that?"

"Do we know anything about the profile?" I ask.

"Just that it's another man, entirely different from Nathan Kelly. Not a relative."

"Oh, my God," I murmur.

I feel numb. The room starts to spin.

It's the confirmation I've been fighting for all this time.

"I think the conclusion that the women had been with another man prior to being with Kelly is faulty, even if we suspense the disbelief and go with their theory that it was a coincidence," Parker says. "The DNA was too intact. And these women had been kept on Kelly's property for more than a month each. I think the narrative that there was a second killer was inconvenient. And when Kelly confessed to everything, they had an easy way out," Parker says. "You were right. There is a second killer that knows Nathan Kelly personally."

I sit there, soaking in the words.

I've struggled so long to make something happen. Parker believed me, and he did the rest. He had the connections and the authority. I laugh.

"What?" Parker asks, furrowing his brow, unsure why I'm laughing.

"I just can't believe it," I say. "It was right there the

whole time. They knew. They *knew* there was someone else and didn't *do* anything."

"Remember when I said the system isn't perfect and I see how it works now?" Parker asks. "You'd be horrified how often this happens. I imagine those detectives were eager to put an end to the panic. And they had a guy confessing to everything and swearing that no one else was involved. And they had nothing else to go on."

"What do we do now?" I ask.

"We need to get a match for that DNA profile. They're running it through CODIS now. They're also seeing if we can get any matches from the genealogy companies. If we had a suspect, we could get a piece of trash they tossed in a trash can and send it in to be analyzed," Parker says. "Otherwise, we'd need a warrant."

"We don't have a suspect, though, do we?" I ask.

"There's the catch. Right now, even though there's evidence that another man was with two of Kelly's victims, we don't have much else to supplement that," Parker says.

"We just wait for another body to turn up?" I ask.

"Well, right now, they're also testing any DNA found on the most recent victim to see if it matches the profile found on those two Oklahoma victims. That would be the smoking gun. There would be no way to deny that someone else was consistently involved with Nathan Kelly and the murders."

"How long will that take?" I ask.

"They'll rush it, but I'm not sure."

"God," I say.

I think about another victim turning up. The idea is horrifying. Waiting seems impossible. How do we just sit on our hands right now?

"Everyone is going to do everything they can," Parker says. "I've talked to Wilson. He's got guys on it. All the campgrounds are being staked out every night. If someone is abducted, they'll see it. They'll chase the guy down."

I think about how no one stopped Kelly the night he drove off with Gloria in the bed of his truck, tucked up under the camper. No one the highway would have had any idea.

"Tell them to look for a truck with a camper," I say.

"Already did," Parker says. He gives me a smile. "You were right, Josephine."

"As nice as that is to hear, I don't think it'll mean much until we catch this guy."

"I understand," Parker says. "But for now, let me take you to lunch."

I'm taken aback by the suggestion. He smiles at me.

"It's good work," he says.

"Well, you did most of that," I say.

"You pointed me in the right direction," he says. "Let me get changed and we can go."

I nod and wait for Parker to get changed. I stroke the top of Ghost's head and he looks back at me, checking in. I smile at him and tell him he's a good boy, giving him a kiss on the side of his face.

"He's a good dog," Parker says as he emerges from the bathroom in a shirt and jeans.

"Casual attire today?" I ask.

"I'll come back and get my suit before we go back in," Parker assures me. "You can't think I wear the monkey suit all the time."

"I was starting to," I say.

He smiles at me and gestures for me to follow him.

Just then, I feel a buzz in my pocket. My phone. I pluck it out and check the notifications.

An email.

And the sender is listed as Robert Copperweight.

I slow down and stop, staring at the phone.

It feels like the bottom has just fallen out. My heart beats faster. I'm overwhelmed by emotion.

"You coming?" Parker asks.

I read the subject of the email.

Congratulations on the book. I always knew you would do great things.

My breathing picks up and I feel myself on the verge of a panic attack. Ghost paws at my leg and I look down at him. I reach for him, petting his head.

I glance up from my phone and see Parker waiting for me at the elevator.

And then I tuck my phone back into my pocket and walk quickly to catch up with Parker.

TWENTY-FIVE

I FIND my mind drifting as Parker talks, food between us, back at the bar we sat at last night. Ghost rests under the table, his warm weight on my foot. It's the only thing that keeps me somewhat tethered to the present moment.

My mind races and I see the subject line of Robert's email like a neon sign above Parker's head. It takes everything inside me—every ounce of self-control I've ever mustered in my life—not to pull my phone out in the middle of his sentence and read that email.

There is absolutely no reason I should care what Robert has to say.

And part of me is so enraged that he had the nerve to reach out to me. Now, of all times.

The great moment of feeling vindicated was followed immediately by his email, crushing every bit of joy I might have gotten out of knowing that there was a second man in that truck.

"Are you okay?" Parker asks when I don't respond at the right moment.

I focus my eyes back on him and shake my head.

"I'm fine," I tell him with a smile.

"Is it the notification you got earlier?" Parker asks.

The question is jarring. He can read me like a book.

"You paused in the hallway and ever since you've had a worried look on your face," Parker goes on.

"It is, yeah," I say. "It was Robert."

"Robert who left you in South Dakota?" Parker asks, seeming as shocked as I am that Rob would have the nerve to show his face around here.

"That one," I say.

"What did it say?" he asks and takes a bite of his burger.

"I don't know," I say. "I didn't see anything besides the subject. I haven't opened it."

"I know it's none of my business," Parker says. "But you deserve a lot better than that guy." He takes a drink of his iced tea and wipes his hands with a napkin. He rests his elbows on the table and looks at me with those eyes that seem to pry right into my deepest secrets. "But," he says. "I'm going to give you advice anyway."

I smile, somewhat sadly.

"I'm up for some advice," I say.

"Good," he says. "My advice is to delete that before you can read it. Because the moment you read it, he gets what he wants. A connection with you. You're a good person, Josephine. You have a heart too big for your own good. You'll answer him if you open that email. And then he'll have you right where he wants you. And, this might be harsh, but never forget where he left you."

Parker takes another bite of his burger.

I know he's right. I know that if I read that email, I'll respond. Parker is completely spot on.

"There's a little part of you that's angry," Parker says after taking another drink of tea. "And you should be. You should be more angry than anything. He left you at a moment when you needed someone more than ever in your life. You can't trust him. Someone who doesn't think twice about dumping a girl at a psych ward to fend for herself is someone that is capable of way more damage than that. And I like you, Josephine. I really do. You're a nice girl. You're a good person. And I know that all of this is going to fall on deaf ears, but Robert isn't. If you want to be with Robert, you will forever be stooping to get on the same level with him. He will never rise to meet you where you're at. And you're at the top right now. So think about what you'll sacrifice to be with him. You already sacrificed enough for him." Parker glances under the table. "And Robert doesn't deserve to set eyes on that dog. He doesn't deserve to see that."

Suddenly, I feel emotional. Not angry, even though Parker's right that I should feel angry.

I feel so much sadness that I'm afraid it's going to swallow up the whole room. That it's going to follow me forever. And that's what Robert is: a sadness that follows me.

It means nothing to him to leave me again. I can't love like that. When I love, I give someone everything I've got. And he doesn't deserve to take that with him again, leaving me to claw it back for years, just trying to get back all the scattered parts of me.

I look up at Parker.

"Thank you," I say, my voice slightly choked up. I swipe at a tear on my right cheek and give Ghost a rub on his head under the table. "Sincerely," I add.

Parker just nods.

"I call it like I see it," Parker says.

It's one of the most refreshing things about him. He shoots straight. I've known so many people who didn't. Only knowing Parker for a few days feels better than any of the time I spent with Robert. Robert was never a friend to me. Not really.

Parker is steady.

Robert was a hurricane.

And within the email on my phone is the distinct possibility for him to come in and tear my life up again. I know I didn't have to go with him to Arizona. I didn't have to do drugs with him. I felt like if I didn't, I'd lose him. And that was way more pressure than he could have ever put on me with his words.

I would have done anything to make him stay.

Everyone has left.

Whether by choice or by death or just circumstance, they're all gone. Unreachable in one way or another.

"We better get back to the station," Parker says as he finishes his burger. "You should get a to-go box." He points at my half-eaten burger and fries and flags down a waitress to get a box. He pays the bill and the three of us head out. We stop by the hotel for him to change into something more professional.

Once back at the police station, things have picked up and there's a hustle to what everyone is doing that I didn't expect to walk into.

"What's going on?" I ask Parker.

"Hang on," he says, and goes over to Wilson to find out what's going on.

I watch as he talks to the other agents. All of them are animated. He comes back over to me quickly.

"A girl went missing last night," Parker says. She and a friend were driving out of town and had car trouble. They stayed at the closest campground. One of them went to the bathroom and never came back." Parker walks over to the group of guys again and grabs a piece of paper, he brings it back over to me and holds it up.

A chill runs through me.

I can see her, hesitantly checking out of the hotel last night, her friend assuring her that nothing was going to go wrong.

"Oh, my God," I say. "I know her."

Parker looks at me with a furrowed brow.

"They checked out of the hotel last night. They were staying in our hotel."

"Her friend reported it as soon as she realized her friend, Amber, wasn't coming back. She spotted a truck with a camper on the back of it heading out of the camp-ground parking lot. It was dark, she didn't get the color."

"It's him," I say. "It's the second DNA profile."

"My thoughts exactly," Parker says.

TWENTY-SIX

THE DAY IS SPENT TRYING to get any possible lead on the truck with the camper on the back of it. It makes me think of my childhood. Five different guys in the trailer park we lived in had campers on their trucks. My family included.

It was something I never thought about until that night Gloria went missing.

There was a guy that lived across from us that always gave me the creeps. He got arrested for child pornography before I graduated from high school. Jordan always had a weird feeling about the guy. He would watch us play in the sprinkler when we were kids, staring just a little too long. My mom kept an eye on him. My dad even more so. And the guy had a truck with a camper on it.

"You keep clear of that guy," my dad said to me one morning, dropping me off at school. He was between jobs so I didn't have to catch the bus for a while. I loved riding to school with him in the morning. He was sober and he'd talk to me. "He's a predator," my dad said.

I remember wondering what a predator was. I didn't ask. My only reference was the movie. I imagined the neighbor transforming into an alien monster at night, stalking through the trailer park. The thought was enough to keep me from going out at night, and it sure made me keep an eye on him when I was outside.

Me and another kid got teased in junior high. Both of our families only had one vehicle. A camper truck. I was teased relentlessly about it when it hit the news that Nathan Kelly had a camper truck. He was in custody by then, but kids are cruel.

After what I saw that night, I always wondered about every single one we passed. Who the person driving was. What cargo they had. I wondered how many people my parents and I passed on the road that were kidnapping women or kids.

"I'd kill anyone that hurt you, Joey," my dad told me one morning on the way to school.

I knew he meant it, too.

If anything had ever happened to me like that, I know my dad would have found a place for a body to go. As I stare at the picture of Amber, I wonder if she has anyone willing to do that for her.

"Her parents are on their way up here. The other girl, Jamie, has her sister coming up," Parker says when he catches me staring at the picture.

"There was a guy that lived in my neighborhood

when I was a kid," I tell Parker. "He ended up being a pervert. The criminal kind. He had a camper truck," I say and look up at Parker. "He went to jail. His name was Dwayne Rodgers."

Parker looks at me for a second.

"I wonder if it's him," I say.

"We haven't gotten a match from CODIS. He'd be in that system," Parker says.

"My dad always warned me to stay away from that guy," I say. "He knew he was a creep before anything had even happened."

"Sounds like a good dad," Parker says.

"He could have been," I say.

"Is he dead?" Parker asks.

"Just about," I say. "He lives near Tulsa in a trailer out on a few acres. He doesn't let me come out there. I think he's ashamed of it. And besides, we've lost touch. Become estranged, I guess you might say."

"Well," Parker says. "I hope someday, before it's too late, you get to make it right with him."

"Me, too," I say.

Life is short, I realize. I think about all that I've lost. My dad is still alive, and even though he's a grumpy old drunk who would rather wrestle a pig than have a conversation, I'd like to try to get him to be a part of my life.

"They're getting more information from Jamie right now. She's in a room down the hallway," Parker says, keeping me updated on everything.

"That's good," I say.

"Very," Parker says. "Did you get much sleep last night?"

"Hardly any," I admit.

"Do you want to go back to the hotel?" he asks. "I can come get you if there's an update. Right now, there's not much to go on as far as going after this guy goes."

We've been sitting here most of the day, I realize. And I'm exhausted. I look down at Ghost. I'm sure he wouldn't turn down another nap.

"Yeah, I think I do want to go rest," I tell Parker.

"I'll run you over there," he says. "Let me excuse myself for a bit."

I wait for Parker and I find myself yawning for the first time today. I'm surprised it hadn't happened sooner.

Finally, he comes and gets us and we go out to the car. I'm quiet on the drive back and he drops me and Ghost off at the door.

"See you later," Parker says. "I'll keep you posted."

"Thank you," I say.

I let Ghost go to the bathroom and then we head into the hotel and upstairs to our room. Once inside, I change into my pajamas again. Ghost snuggles up with me on the bed and we sleep. I find it much easier to fall asleep now, during the day. It feels like nothing bad will happen if the sun is out. Like I won't miss anything crucial.

When I wake up, it's dark.

I check my phone and there are no messages from Parker, which surprises me. I send one to him.

How's it going?

He doesn't respond.

After a few minutes, I wonder if he's in the middle of the shit. Maybe they got called out. They went to the place where this guy is keeping women. Maybe he's in a shoot-out right now. The thought makes me sick.

I think about sending another message, but right around that time, there's a knock at the door.

I get up and go to answer it, standing on my tiptoes to look through the peephole. I see Parker, looking worried. When I open the door, he clears his throat.

"What's happening?" I ask. "Is there any news?"

"I can't say," Parker says.

"What's wrong? Come in," I say.

Parker steps into the dark room and I switch on the lights.

"I have bad news," Parker says. He puts his hands on his hips and paces. "Wilson wants you out." He looks at me.

"What? Why?" I ask.

"He really appreciates what you've done and the direction it's taken things, but he's afraid we're at a critical point where you being a journalist might interfere with things," Parker says. "I tried to talk him out of it. He wouldn't listen. You've met him," he says with a frustrated laugh.

"I don't understand," I say.

"I did everything I could," Parker says. "He's got a flight for you for the morning for wherever you need to go."

Parker paces some more.

"Fuck," I mutter. "I want to finish this."

"I know," Parker says. "I want you to get to see this through."

"There's no other option?" I ask.

"I'm trying to come up with one," Parker says. "Wilson has the final say, though. I can't buck him on this. I don't know what to do."

He looks desperate.

I'm crushed by the fact that I have to leave now. I don't want to. There's so much unfinished.

"I'll think of something," he says. "Take it easy and I'll get something figured out," Parker assures me, placing his hands on my upper arms. "I've gotta go, but I'll be back."

He heads for the door and I watch as it closes behind him.

I look at Ghost and step over to him, kneeling in front of him and hugging him as tightly as I can.

"I have to know," I tell him with tears in my eyes. "You know that right?" I stroke his head. "You be a good boy, and I'll be back."

I stand up and grab my phone from the nightstand. I open my email app and see Robert's name sitting there at the top of the inbox.

I swipe it and delete it.

And then I get dressed for a cold night out in the woods.

TWENTY-SEVEN

I LEAVE Ghost behind and send a text to Parker.

Check on Ghost in an hour. I'll be back.

He texts back almost immediately.

Where are you going?

He sends a flurry of texts when I don't answer.

I get an Uber to take me to the campground where Jamie and Amber were staying after their car broke down. The driver looks at me in the rearview when he drops me off.

"You sure you want to be here?" he asks.

"I'm sure," I say.

"There's a serial killer that's been targeting women at campgrounds around here," he says.

"I know," I say.

He gives me a look that tells me he thinks I'm nuts. And I'm not entirely sure he's wrong. What I'm doing is crazy. It feels like the beginning of mania. I know what

I'm doing is destructive, and potentially life-threatening. But all I can think about is Jordan and Gloria. All I can think about is finishing this once and for all.

I get out of the car at the campground.

The place is empty.

As soon as I shut the door of my Uber, I'm filled with a sense of dread. As he drives off, I realize how heavy the air is out here. It feels viscous. Thick with the sorrow and pain being dealt here. As I walk across the parking lot to the trail that leads to the campground, I'm struck by how noisy my steps are on the ground.

I hear every leaf and stick and bit of gravel crunch beneath my athletic shoes. They're hardly hiking boots. But I don't intend to be out here for long. I just want to get a look at this guy. I want to get his license plate. It's risky.

Lack of sleep is one of the main things that can trigger mania for me. If I go without it for too long, it stirs something up in my brain. I get out of balance. Mania takes over. I can feel it happening now. The decisions I'm making aren't thought out. I'm heading into the woods to stake out and wait for this guy to show up.

It's dangerous.

I left Ghost behind at the hotel. I would never normally do that.

It feels insane, but even so, I can't stop myself. It's like I'm watching myself do it anyway, unable to control my impulses.

Nothing matters right now but making sure I do right by Gloria and Jordan.

I'm hyper-focused on that as I trek down the trail. I find a spot in the woods where I have a good view of the parking lot and enough brush covering me where I won't be seen. I settle in for a long night.

Cars pass on the nearby road. I can hear them, zipping past with people getting to and from their destinations. As the night goes on, the cars become fewer and farther between. Most people have gone back home. They're in bed. Like I should be right now.

I wait, watching from the woods. My phone buzzes in my pocket, surely messages from Parker.

I don't want to check it right now. I don't want to be lectured or told that I need to come back.

I feel myself slipping higher into a manic state, because even the thought of Ghost alone at the hotel isn't enough to make me want to call it a night and go back.

Finally, around 2:00am, I get up and walk down the trail to find the bathroom.

It's surprisingly clean for a campground bathroom. I wash my hands and open the door to head out. And as I'm coming up the trail, I spot something.

Headlights cutting through the trees.

I squat down and throw myself into the brush. I peer out at the headlights.

The vehicle turns and I see that it's a truck, and sure enough, there's a camper on the back.

I freeze in the trees. I fumble for my cellphone and open the camera.

The truck cruises by my spot and I shoot a picture as it turns, hoping to catch the license plate. But my phone does something I don't expect.

The flash goes off.

Again and again and again in a series of flashes.

I pull my phone down, but it's too late. The truck whips around. The door creaks on its hinges as the driver throws it open. I stand from my spot in the trees and run for the trail. I have nowhere to go but further into the campground. I can't run across the parking lot.

The guy starts to run after me.

I don't dare look back. I run, and run.

My heart thunders. My blood runs hot. I feel like I'm going to explode from terror and anxiety and the fear of being caught like prey.

And then he jerks me by the hair down to the ground. I feel the tearing of my scalp. I scream and he claps a gloved hand around my mouth. When he presses his face against mine, I feel the rough fabric of a ski mask against my cheek.

"Don't fight, bitch," he says in low voice, rough with age.

But I don't listen. I fight.

I'm willing to tear my scalp clean off if I can get away from him. I scream at the sensation of pain and roar against his palm. I bite down on his gloved fingers and he pulls his hand back. With the other hand, he pulls on my hair, tearing the flesh some more.

I hear the sickening sound. It's loud and reminds me of velcro. The sensation is blindingly painful. I see white for a moment.

I struggle to get away from him.

"Let me go!" I shout.

He pulls me by the hair down the trail, back toward the parking lot. I fight, screaming the whole way. But there's no one out here. Everyone is avoiding the campgrounds. The cars on the nearby highway are so loud that anyone beyond that wouldn't hear me in a million years.

I feel myself on the verge of a panic attack.

I know better than just about anyone what's coming.

A torn scalp is the least of my worries.

I'm about to experience hell.

And just as I have that thought, we reach the truck. I scream and kick at him, attempting one last time to get away. He takes me by the hair and slams my head into the tailgate of the truck. It's with such brute force that I don't feel anything but the impact for a moment. Just the pressure of my skull colliding with metal.

The pain comes immediately after.

He slams my head against the tailgate again.

I hear the metal give.

He slams it again. Blood drips into my eye.

And then everything goes dark.

TWENTY-EIGHT

WHEN I WAKE, it's dark.

Below me, I feel the corrugated bed of a pickup. Above me is a camper shell. My head throbs and I reach for it, touching crusted blood on my eye as I do so. I moan and reach for my scalp, recalling everything that just happened.

This can't be real.

My scalp is wet and cold. The blood is beginning to get sticky as it congeals. I can feel the place where the skin is torn.

I close my eyes, praying that when I open them, I'll be somewhere else.

I'll be back in my hotel bed with Ghost next to me.

Ghost. Poor Ghost.

Why did I leave him?

Why did I do this?

I feel myself on the verge of a second panic attack. I want to sob uncontrollably.

I tell myself I can't do that. I have to keep it together. I have to find a way to get out of this alive. I remind myself that there are women who got out of this alive. I need to get out of this for Ghost. He won't ever understand if I don't come back. I can't do that to him.

I steel my resolve right then.

And I vow to myself I will get out of this.

I will go home to Ghost.

No matter what it takes.

THE TRUCK KEEPS DRIVING for what seems like forever. The truck bed is starting to hurt my back and I brace myself for what's going to happen when this truck stops and that tailgate opens.

Finally, we hit rougher roads, making me think we're going somewhere exactly like Nathan Kelly's land in Oklahoma. It's just far enough from town that there aren't any neighbors to be nosy or hear someone scream.

The truck slows and comes to a stop. I hear the driver's side door open and brace myself. The truck is still running, though, and he doesn't come to open the tailgate. Instead, he comes back to the truck and gets inside. He pulls forward several yards and then comes to a stop and gets out again.

He's opening and closing a gate, I realize.

We're here.

There's no coming back from this. He is going to kill me.

I tell myself to calm down. I have to keep my wits.

There's a way out of this. Two other women found a way out of this.

The truck drives slowly up a hill. I feel the gravitational shift. And finally, the truck comes to a complete stop and the driver shuts off the engine.

The tailgate opens and dawn light pours in. Before I can push myself up on my elbows, I'm being dragged by my ankles out of the truck. I scream as I fly off the tailgate and hit my head when I land. I curl into the fetal position, dumbstruck by the pain in my scalp.

A boot lands squarely in my spine and I cry out.

"Get up, bitch," the man says. His voice is low, gravely. Like it's been marred by years of smoking. The guy has to be older. If he was operating with Nathan Kelly, he's got to be in his fifties or sixties.

I can outrun this guy in the right circumstances. I just need the right circumstances.

I roll over and push myself up. He kicks me again in the gut, knocking the wind out of me and I slip back into the mud. It fills the spaces between my fingers and I struggle to get a foothold.

"Get up," he says again.

I do it quickly, sure that he'll kick me again if I don't say 'how high' when he tells me to jump.

My whole body hurts as I stand.

"Stand up straight," he says.

He's still wearing the ski mask. He walks around me.

He's a little taller than average. Not a huge guy. He's strong, though. I've learned that the hard way.

I look around, taking in my surroundings. There are trees everywhere. Behind him, there's a shed. And not too far from the shed, there's a cabin.

This is it. This is where he takes them.

"Go," he says, pointing to the shed.

I look around, thinking about running.

"Don't even think about it," he says.

He grabs my hair and points my head down at the ground. I grit my teeth at the pain, but I don't make a sound. I don't want to give him the satisfaction.

He takes me to the shed. There's a padlock on the door and he pulls out a keyring. He opens it and throws the door open. Light pours in and I see her.

Amber.

She's stripped down to her underwear. Just a bra and panties. There are welts all over her skin and her eyes are wide, like a terrified animal's, when she sees the door open. I make eye contact with her and I see that she recognizes me.

I want to tell her that I'm going to get us out of this. I will her to understand that.

I look at her wrist and see that she has one wrist zip-tied to a pipe. There's another pipe on the other side of the shed. He walks me over to it and ties my hand to it. He pushes a bucket to me.

"Piss and shit in that," he says. "I'll come get it."

And then he leaves the shed.

Amber and I are silent, neither of us daring to speak for a long time.

I strain my ears, and I hear the sound of the cabin screen door open and close. I turn to Amber.

"It's okay," I whisper.

Her breathing grows rapid. There are tears in her eyes.

"How can you say that?" she asks.

"It will be," I assure her. "The FBI is going to be here any minute."

"Why do you think that?" she asks.

"They're going to be looking for me."

Amber doesn't seem to get any solace from that. She begins to cry softly.

"We have to work together," I tell her.

She doesn't respond.

I slowly sit down on the floor of the shed. My whole body hurts. I feel as bad as Amber looks, and I imagine I don't look any better.

She stops crying after a while and her breathing sounds more natural. I try to talk to her again.

"I remember you," I say. "From the hotel."

"I remember you, too," she says quietly.

"Amber," I say. She looks over at me. "We're going to get out of here. We are going to be the last women in this shed."

She nods her head, but she lacks conviction. She wants it to be true, though.

That's all I need right now.

I just need her to want to believe we can do this.

Right after I say that, there's a rattling at the door. The sound of a key unlocking the lock. The door goes wide, and our masked captor walks in with two paper plates. He drops one in front of me and one in front of Amber. On each of them is a scoop of wet dog food.

I stare at it.

"You'll get hungry enough for it," he says.

I glance over at Amber and she's picking up wet pieces and shoving them in her mouth. I look away when I see the shame in her eyes.

He stares at her, watching her eat.

He laughs.

And then he turns around and heads out of the shed, closing the doors behind him.

We're surrounded by dark and cold, and all I can hear is the sound of Amber chewing the chunks of dog food.

For a split second, I think I'm dreaming.

There's no way this is real.

But when I open my eyes again, I'm still in this dark, cold shed. I can still hear Amber chewing. I push the plate in front of me away. I don't want it. I don't want to eat here. I want to be gone before that even becomes something I'll consider.

I try to think of something. The day wears on and I

find myself needing to pee. I barely manage to get my pants off to use the bucket and it takes me forever to get them back on. Amber is quiet, sleeping most of the day.

And then around dinner time, he's back.

I feel my body stiffen as the shed doors open.

Amber sits up quickly, brought to attention by the sound. She shrinks back into the corner when he heads for her with a knife. He slips it under the zip tie and frees her, grabbing her by the hair.

"No, please," she says.

She begins to cry and he doesn't even hesitate for a second.

She makes eye contact with me, and I know exactly what's about to happen to her. My stomach turns and I taste bile on the back of my tongue. He shuts the door behind him and she begs all the way to the cabin.

I throw up twice into the bucket.

TWENTY-NINE

I WAIT for Amber to come back, and the darkness inside the shed starts to get to me. I see shapes in the darkness, dancing on the walls. The walls themselves seem to breathe, in and out. I'm not sure how much time passes, but all I can imagine is that it's the longest few hours of Amber's life.

God, I hope Parker is coming after me.

I know he is. Of course he is.

The only problem is I don't think he knows where to go.

I think about him telling me that Wilson didn't want me on the inside anymore. Maybe they figured it out. Maybe they had some sensitive information Wilson was afraid I would compromise. Maybe he didn't think I could pass up a good story.

I pray they know something, and I haven't prayed in years.

I'm not even sure I believe God is listening. I find it hard to believe he'd allow a man like this to exist if God were real. It's a bleak thought on the heels of a prayer.

I need some way to contact Parker. I need to call 911. And I need to know where I am.

Finally, I hear the screen door open and slam. Amber whimpers as the man walks her back to the shed. He throws the doors open, and it's then that I realize he didn't bother locking them when he took her inside.

It's a complacency that could come back to bite him. He's sure of himself out here.

I find myself shrinking back when he opens the door. Once again, he's masked. He takes Amber by the hair and zip-ties her once again to the pipe on the other side of the shed. She whimpers and cowers like a dog, scooting as far as she can away from him. He brings a hand down and strokes her hair and face. She cringes, trying to turn herself inside out to get away from him.

He turns his attention to me and I try my hardest not to react physically. I don't want to give him the satisfaction of seeing me scared. I steady my breathing and he kneels down in front of me. I can barely see his eyes behind the mask, but I can feel the heat of his breath.

"I wanna talk to you," he says, and then with a quick flick of the knife in his other hand, he frees my bound wrist. I reach for it instinctively, rubbing it with my other hand. "Get up and walk."

I do as he says, and outside the shed, I take a moment

to look around. I try not to let him see. In the distance, there's some sort of tower. The day is cloudy and dark and I can make out the faintest hint of red light at the top of it.

A blinking light at the top of a tower. It's a valuable piece of data. I fight the voice that says there are probably hundreds of them.

I strain my ears to listen, and I hear the faintest rumble of a highway in the distance. It's got to be miles. At least five, probably more.

Five miles. I can make it five miles.

I don't know if Amber can, though.

He prods my back when I slow down, processing my thoughts.

"Go on," he says.

We get to the cabin and when the screen door creaks on its hinge, I feel dread. I know what just happened to Amber. This guy is old, though, I realize. That isn't what this is about.

He shoves me into the dimly lit cabin and I stumble slightly.

The walls are log. The place is hand-built. This isn't commercial construction. He did this all himself.

"Sit," he says, gesturing to the dining table. He goes into the kitchen and gets me a bottle of water. He hands it to me. "Who are you?" he asks.

"What does it matter who I am?" I ask, defiant.

"I don't think you wanna make this more complicated than it already is," he says. "Besides, if I turn on the news,

I'm pretty sure I can find out from them. I'd much rather hear it from you."

I inhale deeply.

"Who are you?" I ask him. "Don't you think it's fair that you tell me that?"

He laughs behind the mask.

"Now, why would I go and do something like that?"

"It's only fair," I suggest. "I bet Kelly would go for it."

The mention of Kelly makes the man's posture shift from someone in control to someone on edge.

"Kelly's an idiot," he says.

"Didn't you work with him?" I ask. "You were there the night he abducted his first victim. Was it your first victim, too?"

"No. She wasn't," the man says evenly.

"How many were there before her?" I ask.

"Enough to be smart about it," he says.

"I don't think Kelly wanted to give you any credit," I say.

He laughs at that.

"You think you can get under my skin talking about Nathan Kelly like you know him?"

"I know him pretty well," I say. "Maybe better than you."

"You know him real well, you think," the man says. "Well, let me tell you something. You don't know shit, Joey."

My blood runs cold. My heart almost stops in my chest. Every ounce of bravado that I had is gone. I'm terrified. I'm in the woods, looking at Nathan Kelly at the back of that truck. The memory is brief. It's only a split second.

But right before everything goes black, the second man in the truck turns.

And I'd know him anywhere.

The man in front of me pulls off his mask.

He's aged, but I recognize him in an instant.

My dad.

THIRTY

"DRINK YOUR WATER," he says.

My chest caves in, my flesh and bones weigh on my lungs and I can't breathe. The room spins. I feel like a hand is squeezing my heart and the muscle hurts worse than it ever has. It's not like a panic attack I've experienced before. This time, I know I'm dying.

He grabs the bottle from in front of me and opens it, pressing it to my mouth and forcing me to drink.

I gulp. I have to keep my wits about me, I remind myself. But the tiny voice is drowned out by so many other thoughts.

You.

I look at him when he brings it down.

I realize then that I'm trembling.

"What?" I manage. "What's happening?"

"Exactly what you think is happening, Joey. Don't be dumb," he says. "You were never a dumb kid."

"I knew it was you," I say, sounding like a raving lunatic. "I saw your face that night."

"When you and Jordan went camping," he finishes for me, almost bored with the story. "That's how I knew Gloria would be there. She was the only one that wasn't just an opportunity. I'd had my eye on her."

I think back on all the times that Gloria would pick me up. My dad would stand there and talk to her in the window of her car.

He wasn't being nice. He was sizing her up for the kill.

My mind reels.

I think back to all the nights he didn't come home. Nights that my mom cursed him because she thought he was at the bar.

"Why?" I ask, my voice barely a croak.

"I don't know what to tell you, kiddo," he says. "This is just who I am. I suppose you'd know more about it than I would."

All this time interviewing a serial killer while I had the same kind of blood running through my veins.

"You left us," I say. "Is this why?"

"Things got complicated," he says. "I met Nate at a bar one night. We both had our eye on the same girl, and I could tell Nate was like me. The way he looked at her told me everything. He was a predator, too. I got that girl to the truck with us. Then we took her out somewhere remote and both had our way with her. Then I killed her. Showed him how to slit a girl's throat."

As he says it, the years shake themselves off his voice. Suddenly, I'm able to recognize it through all that aging and all those cigarettes. It's my dad's voice. The voice of someone I trusted. The *only* person I trusted besides Jordan. And he took her away from me.

"After that, Kelly and I killed together a few times. When the heat was on, I knew I needed to get outta there. I hated to leave you," he says. "I wanted to take you from your mom and take you with me."

The thought is chilling.

Instead of being raised by an alcoholic, I could have been raised by a serial killer.

He gives me a sympathetic look that makes me feel like he means it. That he's sorry for leaving. It's almost comical and I laugh.

"What's funny?" he asks.

"That you'd think taking a kid on the road while you found women to kill would be any kind of a life for a child," I say. "Mom always said you were selfish. Maybe she was right."

"Your mom didn't know how much I loved you, Joey," he says, more emotion in his voice than I've ever heard any sociopath or psychopath use. I wonder if he really feels it or if its just affect. "She was a nag and a meddler. She couldn't stand that you and I were closer than she was with you. I could see it in the way she looked at me. And she was always jealous of you," he adds. "She always thought you were gonna steal the spotlight away from her."

I swallow, unsure of how to respond.

"I'm trying to process all of this," I say.

He nods silently.

"Did you know it was me last night?" I ask.

"Not 'til this morning," he says.

"How did this all happen?" I ask, more to myself than to him.

"This is just who I am, Joey. And in a way, it's who you are, too."

"No," I say. "Don't say that."

"You got the same blood running through your veins as I do," he says.

"Not on this," I say. "You can't keep doing this."

"You want me to quit? Turn myself in?" he asks with a laugh.

He's quiet for a moment.

"Why didn't Nathan Kelly turn you in?"

"We swore we would never rat each other out," he says. "We were both drawn to this and did some of the greatest work together. But why take that away from someone just because you get caught?" Then he smirks. "Plus, Nathan knew if he ever breathed a word of my involvement, I'd kill his whole family."

The way he says it sends ice through my veins.

He really means it.

He would kill all of them.

This man that I love would kill in cold blood.

Has killed in cold blood.

"You can't keep doing this," I say.

"Stay," he says. "Help me be better, Joey."

I don't say anything.

Nothing quite like a parent asking you to stop them from killing people.

The whole situation is surreal.

"Are you going to kill me, too?" I ask.

"Don't be ridiculous," he says. "At least, not if you don't do anything stupid." He adds the last part with a wicked grin.

"Like try to leave?" I ask.

"That would probably do it," he says. "You'd go back to your friends at the FBI and let 'em know where I'm at. I can't have that, Joey."

"Stop calling me that," I say.

"You loved that nickname when you were a kid," he says.

"I think *you* loved it," I say. "You always wished I was a boy."

He's quiet for a moment.

"Did you want me to follow in your footsteps?" I ask, horrified by the thought.

He raises his eyebrows and shrugs. Like the thought had definitely crossed his mind at some point. I feel sick.

"Do you hate women?" I ask.

I think about the way the victims were treated. I try to imagine my own father doing that. The man who kept me safe from our creepy neighbor. I can't quite picture it.

"I never hated you," he says.

But the sentence is loaded. I know what the omission means.

"I guess I was trying to work out my frustrations with your mother," he says. "You know she's difficult."

"Did you know she died?"

His face is expressionless.

"I just wish I could have been there when she did," he says coldly.

I know he means it. This man provided for me as a kid and took me with him to work. He's a monster.

"Please let Amber go," I say.

"And let her talk?" he asks. "I already got one that's talked to the cops by now."

"Drop her off somewhere far from here. Scare her. She won't talk," I say. The words come out like I'm pleading.

"And what about you?" he asks.

"I'll stay," I tell him. "I'll help you be better."

It's a lie.

I have no intention of that, and even if I did, it wouldn't work.

He looks at me with a softness in his eyes.

"You'd do that?" he asks.

I nod vigorously and he seems to think about this possibility.

"I'm sorry, Joey," he finally says. "But that ain't gonna work for me."

THIRTY-ONE

HE TAKES me back to the shed, none the worse for wear physically, but mentally spent. He zip ties my wrist to the pipe and he doesn't use any gentleness.

I need him to trust me.

But I don't think that's going to happen.

Amber and I don't talk all night. My dad brings us food—dog food like before—and I'm hungry, but I refuse to eat it. I look over at Amber, watching her devour it with her fingers. She's starving. It's been days since she had a real meal. I look at what he's reduced her to. What he's reduced so many other women to.

There's a tiny sliver of me that entertains the idea of staying.

I miss him. I miss the man I knew when I was a kid. But facts creep in. All that while, he was murdering women. He'd be gone all night doing God knows what and come back to us, like nothing had happened.

How could he?

The idea of being so duplicitous is astonishing to me. You hear it all the time with serial killers. How they led an entirely separate life that their family had no idea about. But the full impact of how shocking that is will never hit you until you're in the middle of it.

You can think you know someone—really know them—and be wrong. You can live with someone day after day for *years* and not know who they really are.

I look at Amber as the last light of day fades.

"We're gonna get out of here," I whisper in the darkness. "Trust me."

TWO DAYS PASS LIKE THAT. I finally break down and eat the dog food. It's cold and slimy. It makes me glad that Ghost eats dry and makes me rethink his entire diet. The thought of him saddens me. I wish I was with him right now. I can't think about how he's doing. We're bonded at the hip and have been since he was a puppy.

I should never have left him.

But the idea of Ghost just fuels the fire inside me. I have to survive this.

I need a phone. I need the internet.

When it comes time for dinner, he brings me inside and I realize that now's my chance. I don't know how many more I'll have and I have zero doubt that he'd be happy to get rid of me, regardless of whatever he feels for me as his daughter. At this point, I'm a liability.

When we get inside, the conversation turns casual.

I bring up better times, memories from when I was a kid.

"Do you remember that?" I ask with a laugh.

"I do," he says with a smile. "You were a good kid, Joey."

I'm silent for a moment.

"I'll be back," he says.

He excuses himself to go to the bathroom. I'm alone in the kitchen. I groan when I realize he's taken his phone with him. So much for that.

My wrists are bound to each other, but my eyes dart to the drawers next to the stove.

A knife. I need a knife.

I move quietly but quickly. I pull open one drawer after the other until I find the one with the silverware and I pull out a steak knife. And then I dart for the door.

I open it as quietly as I possibly can and slip out into the evening air.

I run to the shed. I realize that if I don't get out of here right now, I never will.

Once again, out of complacency, he left it unlocked. With my hands still bound together I throw it open. I run over to Amber, who looks at me with wide eyes.

"Undo this," I tell her. "Quick!"

She takes the knife and starts sawing. Finally, the

neon yellow zip ties pop open. I grab the knife from her and free her.

"Run," I whisper.

And it's then that I hear the screen door open.

HE COMES out of the cabin with a roar and a rifle in hand. He takes a shot at us as we sprint for the woods.

"By the driveway!" I tell Amber.

She follows me, struggling to keep up in her bare feet. I can hear her breathing. She sounds like a wild animal, running from something bigger with sharper teeth. I know I sound the same.

He shoots after us as we head into the thicker part of the woods. I can hear him keeping pace.

"Come on!" I shout to Amber as she starts to lag behind.

I hear her struggling. I reach back and grab her hand.

"We have to go, now!" I tell her through ragged breaths.

And we run.

The footfalls behind us get softer and softer. And we run through rough terrain for what I'm sure is an hour. Maybe we've covered a mile, I realize.

We keep going, our pace slowing. And I don't hear him behind us.

"Come on," I whisper. "We have to keep going."

There are tears in Amber's eyes.

"Do you want to see Jamie again? Your family?" I ask. "They're waiting for you."

She nods, my words seeming to steel her for another mile. We keep going.

I keep us close to the dirt drive that leads into my father's land. I keep an eye out, waiting for his truck to come barreling down the road, but it doesn't. I wonder if he's just behind us, quiet as a mouse. The possibility is there. He knows the woods. He's been hunting women through them for decades.

I wonder how many there are.

All I know is that I refuse to let Amber and I become the next two.

Night falls. Amber begins to shiver, still clad in only her underwear.

I realize the knife is still in my hand. I've had a vice grip on it all afternoon. My knuckles ache around it, but I squeeze it even tighter. It's all we've got right now.

"How much further do you think?" Amber asks.

"I'd say we're still miles from the highway," I tell her.

Just then, I hear it.

A distinct sound. Something I thought only belonged to Nathan Kelly. But there it is, drifting through the woods.

A whistle.

I freeze and my heart races in my chest. He's still after us.

"Go!" I whisper, and we start crashing through the

woods again. Amber falls and I help her up. I can practically feel him breathing down our necks.

And it's just then that I see the headlights.

They're coming up the drive, one car followed by another. SUVs with law enforcement setups. I stand there, on the edge of the woods, much like I did the night Gloria was taken. I start to laugh hysterically. I grab Amber's hand and I pull her out into the road.

I throw myself out there and I almost get hit. But the car in front of me stops dead in its tracks, and someone gets out, racing to my side.

He wraps me in a hug, embracing me tightly.

It's Parker.

THIRTY-TWO

I START to sob and he holds me tighter.

"How did you find us?" I ask.

"Someone saw the truck. He stopped at a gas station and they thought he was suspicious. They called it in and we got the plate from the security camera," Parker says. He pulls away. "Are you hurt?"

"I'm fine. Amber needs medical attention," I say.

Another FBI agent is giving her a blanket and taking her to the back of his car behind us.

"He's out there," I say.

"We're on it," Parker assures me. "Get in the car," he says authoritatively. And I do as I'm told.

I hear gunshots. Multiple gunshots. Like a gunfight.

My stomach clenches and threatens to empty the contents of my stomach onto my lap. They're shooting at my dad. The last person with any biological connection to me.

I sit there silently, listening to each shot.

A man yells out. *Cries* out.

And then the gunshots cease.

Parker sits silently in the car beside me.

"He's my father," I say.

Parker looks at me in the darkness of the car.

"What?" he asks.

"You heard me," I say. "He and Kelly worked together."

"Jesus Christ. How is that possible?"

"That night that I saw Gloria get abducted, it was him in the cab of the truck. I always knew it," I tell Parker. "I just couldn't see it. My mind wouldn't let me see it."

Parker sits, stunned into silence for a moment.

"Let's get you out of here," he says.

He gets out of the car and makes a phone call, then slips back inside. He and the car behind him turn around on the narrow dirt drive, and then we head back into town.

THE DRIVE IS LONG. An hour at least. I just stare straight ahead, most likely in shock.

Parker doesn't bother trying to make small talk, and I'm grateful for that. Finally, I say something.

"Where's Ghost?" I ask.

"He's fine," Parker says. "Actually just hanging out in my hotel room."

I smile at the thought.

"Thank you," I say. The mania is still crawling beneath my skin. "I need to sleep," I tell him.

"We'll get you back to the hotel," he says.

When we get back to the hotel and up to the eighth floor, I walk as quickly as I can down the hallway, eager to see Ghost. Parker unlocks the door and the dog comes bounding out. He tackles me to the ground with kisses. His tail wags wildly.

"He was devastated that you were gone," Parker says.

I say nothing, but I cling to Ghost like my life depends on it.

Because it does.

THE NEXT FEW days are a blur.

I stay mostly in the hotel room and Parker updates me each night over dinner at the bar across the street.

It turns out that my dad and Nathan Kelly owned the land in Alaska for years under false names. The plan was that if either of them got caught, the other would head north. And that's exactly what my dad did in 2003 when Kelly got arrested.

He really was scared of my father. It turned out that Peter Larson was the brains of the operation. He got

Kelly to do a lot of his dirty work. Caught and with nowhere to turn, my dad spilled his guts.

"I just can't believe I never knew," I say to Parker after we finish dinner. Ghost sits beneath the table, head resting on my foot. I've gotten a lot of sleep since I got back and the mania is subdued. I know a crash is coming, but I don't want to think about that for now.

"I don't think it's that you didn't know," Parker says. "You did. You had that memory deep inside your mind. I think you protected yourself from it," he says.

I nod. Parker's right.

I did have the memory buried deep in my mind.

I just couldn't reconcile reality with the man I knew as my father.

"It'll make a hell of a sequel," Parker says with a wink.

"Fuck," I mutter. "I hadn't even thought that far."

The media whirlwind will begin soon. I can't imagine how this will go over. Josephine Larson's father turns out to be one-half of the Heartland Hunter, right under her nose.

I laugh.

It can't be worse than what I've experienced in the last couple of weeks.

Parker and I spend the rest of our nights there laughing over dinner. Finally, the night before my flight out of Alaska, we hit the bar one more time.

"You know," he says. "I'm going to miss you."

"I'll miss you, too," I say.

"You delete that email?" he asks.

"I did," I tell him.

I haven't thought of Robert since I got back.

"Good for you," Parker says. He raises a beer bottle to toast. I do the same and we clink glasses.

I just smile at him.

The next morning at the airport, Parker drops me off.

He starts to shake my hand but I insist on a hug instead.

"Until we meet again, Josephine Larson," Parker says.

"Until we meet again, Special Agent Parker," I say.

"I think you can call me Luke now," he adds with a smile.

"See you, Luke," I say.

And Ghost and I watch as he drives off.

The flight home is peaceful. Ghost rests the whole way. We have another layover in Denver, and then we get back to Oklahoma. I call my publisher, not bothering to update them on the biggest bombshell of the whole experience. I tell them I want to take a break before I get back out to California to conduct my next set of interviews.

They're understanding.

Ghost and I walk into my parents' old trailer. I lock the door behind us and collapse on the couch. I don't even bother changing. Ghost climbs on top of me and falls immediately asleep.

I don't want to think about what's happened. I don't even know what kind of time that it'll take to process. But when I sleep that night, I dream about seeing Parker again in a much nicer set of circumstances. As friends.

Ghost snuggles deeper against me in the middle of the night, his warm breath through the blanket waking me up.

I open my eyes and look around the room.

This place where I grew up.

The place where my father raised me.

And the place I came to heal after Robert broke me.

A smile curves my lips and I reach down to pat Ghost.

I'm ready to move on.

I'm ready to start again.

ACKNOWLEDGMENTS

I realize this is a work of fiction and my imagination took liberties with certain things, however, I do finally get to say that all those podcasts I've listened to and ID Discovery shows I've watched have come in handy.

Thanks to my mom who is always my biggest supporter. I couldn't have made this one happen without her. To my family who is always supportive. My friends, who loved this storyline from the beginning. To my wonderful assistant Ann, who is nothing short of magical. To my ARC team for all your reviews, I couldn't do this without each and every one of you. Your time is precious and I'm honored that you exchange it for one of my stories. To my Street Team who go above and beyond, you are the most wonderful group of people I've ever met. You make my job a joy. All of you encourage me constantly to be better and write better.

To my dogs, who, like Ghost, are my constant companion. Penny, you might not have made the cut as a service dog, but you sure are a comfort to me on the worst of days. And to Ellie, who is a bundle of energy and joy no matter what. To Maggie, the happiest little border collie mix you ever met. And finally, to T Bear, the queen that rules them all.

I hope y'all enjoyed the book and I'll catch you in the next one.

ABOUT THE AUTHOR

I started writing when I was 7. The book was called *It Came Floating Up*. It was inspired by many trips to the beach and watching a few too many episodes of *The X-Files* with my grandmother. The book was about a monster lurking in the sargasso seaweed just off the coast of Corpus Christi. In the dedication, I wrote:

To my family, who has been there through everything.

I was 7. If only I'd known then what exactly *everything* would entail.

Since then, I've only gotten more dramatic and more obsessed with *The X-Files* and storytelling.

My books all have one thing in common: they are inspired by some element of truth either in my own life or something I pick out of a headline or a history book. Mostly, though, my writing is inspired by my own experiences and emotions, just blown up on a grander scale with a murder or two to make it exciting.

Just call me the Taylor Swift of psychological thrillers.

JOIN MY NEWSLETTER

Sign up now and get a free horror novella, The Body Snatchers. You'll also get updates, freebies, news about me and my dogs, plus book discounts and sales!

Sign up here:

https://BookHip.com/PZGBMZT

ALSO BY MARNIE VINGE

SHOP NOW

www.marniewritesthrillers.com

Psychological Thrillers

The Getaway

Swingers

For Rosie

I Remember Everything

Cold Blood

Women's Thrillers

The Way It Ends

What We Did That Night

Manspreader

The Blair Graves Files

The Haunting of Solomon House

The Holloway Hoax

The Vampire's Game

One Night in September

Short Horror Collections

Thicker Than Water

In Sheep's Clothing

The Reunion

Romance

Gunshy

www.ingramcontent.com/pod-product-compliance
Lightning Source LLC
Chambersburg PA
CBHW022035240626
47154CB00007B/2422

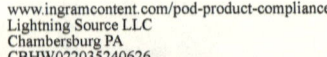